THE BEGINNER'S GOODBYE

The Beginner's Goodbye

a novel by Anne Tyler

Chatto & Windus
LONDON

Published by Chatto & Windus 2012

2 4 6 8 10 9 7 5 3 1

Copyright © Anne Tyler 2012

Published in the United States of America by Alfred A. Knopf in 2012

Anne Tyler has asserted her right under the Copyright, Designs
and Patents Act 1988 to be identified as the author of this work

First published in Great Britain in 2012 by
Chatto & Windus
Random House, 20 Vauxhall Bridge Road,
London SW1V 2SA
www.rbooks.co.uk

Addresses for companies within The Random House Group Limited can be found at:
www.randomhouse.co.uk/offices.htm

The Random House Group Limited Reg. No. 954009

A CIP catalogue record for this book
is available from the British Library

Hardback ISBN 9780701187194
Trade paperback ISBN 9780701187200

The Random House Group Limited supports The Forest Stewardship Council
(FSC®), the leading international forest certification organisation. Our books
carrying the FSC label are printed on FSC® certified paper. FSC is the only forest
certification scheme endorsed by the leading environmental organisations,
including Greenpeace. Our paper procurement policy can be found at:
www.randomhouse.co.uk/environment

MIX
Paper from
responsible sources
FSC

Printed a

The
Beginner's
Goodbye

1

The strangest thing about my wife's return from the dead was how other people reacted.

We were strolling through Belvedere Square, for instance, on an early-spring afternoon when we met our old next-door neighbor, Jim Rust. "Well, what do you know," he said to me. "Aaron!" Then he noticed Dorothy beside me. She stood peering up at him with one hand shielding her forehead from the sun. His eyes widened and he turned to me again.

I said, "How's it going, Jim?"

Visibly, he pulled himself together. "Oh . . . great," he said. "I mean . . . or, rather . . . but of course we miss you. Neighborhood is not the same without you!"

He was focusing on me alone—specifically, on my mouth, as if I were the one who was talking. He wouldn't look at Dorothy. He had pivoted a few inches so as to exclude her from his line of vision.

I took pity on him. I said, "Well, tell everybody hello," and we walked on. Beside me, Dorothy gave one of her dry chuckles.

Other people pretended not to recognize either one of us.

They would catch sight of us from a distance, and this sort of jolt would alter their expressions and they would all at once dart down a side street, busy-busy, much to accomplish, very important concerns on their minds. I didn't hold it against them. I knew this was a lot to adjust to. In their position, I might have behaved the same way. I like to think I wouldn't, but I might have.

The ones who made me laugh aloud were the ones who had forgotten she'd died. Granted, there were only two or three of those—people who barely knew us. In line at the bank once we were spotted by Mr. von Sant, who had handled our mortgage application several years before. He was crossing the lobby and he paused to ask, "You two still enjoying the house?"

"Oh, yes," I told him.

Just to keep things simple.

I pictured how the realization would hit him a few minutes later. *Wait!* he would say to himself, as he was sitting back down at his desk. *Didn't I hear something about . . . ?*

Unless he never gave us another thought. Or hadn't heard the news in the first place. He'd go on forever assuming that the house was still intact, and Dorothy still alive, and the two of us still happily, unremarkably married.

I had moved in by then with my sister, who lived in our parents' old place in north Baltimore. Was that why Dorothy came back when she did? She hadn't much cared for Nandina. She thought she was too bossy. Well, she *was* too bossy. Is. She's especially bossy with me, because I have a couple of handicaps. I may not have mentioned that. I have a crippled right arm and leg. Nothing that gets in my way, but you know how older sisters can be.

Oh, and also a kind of speech hesitation, but only intermittently. I seldom even hear it, myself.

In fact, I have often wondered what made Dorothy select the moment she did to come back. It wasn't immediately after she died, which is when you might expect. It was months and months later. Almost a year. Of course I could have just asked her, but somehow, I don't know, the question seemed impolite. I can't explain exactly why.

One time we ran into Irene Lance, from my office. She's the design person there. Dorothy and I were returning from lunch. Or *I* had had lunch, at least, and Dorothy had fallen into step beside me as I was walking back. And suddenly we noticed Irene approaching from St. Paul. Irene was hard to miss. She was always the most elegant woman on the street, not that that was much of a challenge in Baltimore. But she would have seemed elegant anywhere. She was tall and ice-blonde, wearing a long, flowing coat that day with the collar turned up around her throat and the hemline swirling about her shins in the brisk spring breeze. I was curious. How would a person like Irene handle this type of thing? So I slowed my pace, which caused Dorothy to slow hers, and by the time Irene caught sight of us we were almost at a standstill, both of us waiting to see what Irene would do.

Two or three feet away from us, she stopped short. "Oh . . . my . . . God," she said.

We smiled.

"UPS," she said.

I said, "What?"

"I phoned UPS for a pickup and there's nobody in the office."

"Well, never mind. We're heading back there right now," I told her.

I used the word "we" on purpose, although Dorothy would most likely depart before I entered the building.

But all Irene said was, "Thanks, Aaron. I must be getting Alzheimer's."

And off she went, without another word.

She would *really* have worried about Alzheimer's if she had known what she'd just overlooked.

I glanced over at Dorothy, expecting her to share the joke, but she was pursuing her own line of thought. *"Wild Strawberries,"* she said, in a reflective tone of voice.

"Pardon?"

"That's who Irene reminds me of. The woman in the old Bergman movie—the daughter-in-law, with the skinned-back bun. Remember her?"

"Ingrid Thulin," I said.

Dorothy raised her eyebrows slightly, to show she was impressed, but it wasn't so very difficult to dredge that name up. I had been enamored with Ingrid Thulin since college. I liked her cool, collected air.

"How long do you suppose it will be before Irene does a double take?" I asked Dorothy.

Dorothy merely shrugged.

She seemed to view our situation much more matter-of-factly than I did.

Maybe the reason I didn't ask Dorothy why she had come back when she did was that I worried it would make her ask herself the same question. If she had just sort of *wandered* back, absentmindedly, the way you would return to an old address out of habit, then once I'd brought it up she might say, "Oh! My goodness! I should be going!"

Or maybe she would imagine I was asking what she was doing here. Why she had come back at all, in other words. Like when you ask a houseguest how long he's planning to stay and he suspects you're asking, "When can I hope to be rid of you?" Maybe that was why I felt it wouldn't be polite.

It would kill me if she left. I had already gone through that once. I didn't think I could do it all over again.

She was short and plump and serious-looking. She had a broad, olive-skinned face, appealingly flat-planed, and calm black eyes that were noticeably level, with that perfect symmetry that makes the viewer feel rested. Her hair, which she cut herself in a heedless, blunt, square style, was deeply, absolutely black, and all of a piece. (Her family had come from Mexico two generations before.) And yet I don't think other people recognized how attractive she was, because she hid it. Or, no, not even that; she was too unaware of it to hide it. She wore owlish, round-lensed glasses that mocked the shape of her face. Her clothes made her figure seem squat—wide, straight trousers and man-tailored shirts, chunky crepe-soled shoes of a type that waitresses favored in diners. Only I noticed the creases as fine as silk threads that encircled her wrists and her neck. Only I knew her dear, pudgy feet, with the nails like tiny seashells.

My sister said Dorothy was too old for me, but that was just because I had foolishly told the truth when I was asked. Even though she was eight years my senior—forty-three when she died—she seemed younger, because of that good strong Hispanic skin. Plus, she had enough padding to fill out any lines. You wouldn't really think about age at all, with Dorothy.

My sister also said she was too short for me, and it is undeniable that when Dorothy and I hugged, all the wrong parts of us met. I am six-feet-four. Dorothy was not quite five-one. If you saw us walking down the street together, my sister said, you would take us for a father and child heading off to grammar school.

And too professional, my sister said. Ha! There's a novel objection. Dorothy was a doctor. I work as an editor in my family's publishing firm. Not all that great a disparity, right? What Nandina meant was, too *intent* upon her profession. Too work-obsessed. She left for her office early, stayed late, didn't greet me with my slippers in the evening, barely knew how to boil an egg. Fine with me.

But not with Nandina, evidently.

Maybe it was just a long, long way to travel, and that's why it took Dorothy all those months to come back.

Or maybe she had first tried to do without me, the way I had first tried to do without her—to "get over" my loss, "find closure," "move on," all those ridiculous phrases people use when they're urging you to endure the unendurable. But eventually, she had faced the fact that we simply missed each other too much. She had given in and returned.

That's what I liked to believe.

I've made my sister out to be a tyrant, but she really wasn't. She just wanted the best for me, is why she was so critical. She *saw* the best in me. When a neighbor kid called me Frankenstein, after I got so tall, Nandina told me I resembled Abraham Lincoln. (I pretended to take heart from this, although Abraham Lincoln was not the look I'd been aiming for.) When I admitted to a case of nerves before inviting Tiffy Preveau to the freshman prom, Nandina rehearsed with me for hours, throwing herself into the role of Tiffy so convincingly that I all but lost my tongue around her. "Could—could—could—" I stammered.

"Start with an *H* word," Nandina advised, slipping out of character for a moment.

"How—how would you like—to go to the prom with me?" I asked.

"Why, I'd love to, Aaron!" she said in a burbly, false voice. "But tell me: are you able to dance?"

"Oh, yes."

"Because I really do love to dance, you know. And I'm talking *fast*-dance. I like to go crazy!"

"I can fast-dance," I said.

And I could. Nandina had taught me. Nandina was not exactly a teen success story herself (she stood nearly six feet tall even after shucking off her long banana shoes, and had reached her senior year without attending a single one of her own proms), but she steered me through a series of passable-looking moves. She showed me how to bite my lower lip as if transported by the beat of "Pump Up the Volume," and she positioned my right arm so it seemed less like a broken wing and more like a banner, raised triumphantly as high as she could force it. It worked in my favor that nobody was dancing in that walking-embrace style anymore. I wouldn't need to clasp my partner two-handed or anything like that.

And I should learn to do without all those *C* words, Nandina said. It seemed to her I was piling them on deliberately—"can" and "could," every chance I got.

"That might not be entirely coincidental," I told her. (I spoke almost without a hitch, since she was merely my sister again.)

"See what I mean? You could just as well have used '*ac*cidental' there," she said.

Tiffy turned down my invitation, as it happened. She said she'd already made plans. But still, it was kind of Nandina to offer her help.

I was wrong to use the word "handicaps" earlier. "Differences" would have been more accurate. Really I'm not handicapped in the least.

I may be different from other people but I'm no unluckier. I believe that. Or I'm unluckier but no unhappier. That is probably closer to the truth.

Sometimes I think I am unluckier than other people but much, much happier.

But there I suppose I'm fooling myself, because probably everyone thinks he has some unique claim on happiness.

The weird thing is that, although I have been this way for as long as I can remember, I *feel* myself to be exactly like everyone else. Staring out through the windows of my eyes, I imagine my back to be straight, my neck upright, and my arms of a matching diameter. In actuality, though, since my right foot and calf are pretty much deadweight I have to drag my right leg behind me, and I lean away from that side to counterbalance it, which throws my spine askew. When I'm seated, you might not guess, but then I stand up and I'm listing.

I own a cane, but I keep leaving it places.

And although I have trained myself to let my right arm hang as loosely as possible, it insists on reverting to a tucked position with the hand bent inward, folded sharply at the wrist as if I were a stroke victim. Maybe I *am* a stroke victim; I don't know. I was a perfectly normal two-year-old; then I came down with the flu. After that I wasn't normal anymore.

But I'll bet I would have been left-handed in any case, because I have excellent penmanship and I didn't need to struggle for it. So in that respect I am *not* so unlucky, wouldn't you agree? And I play a wicked game of racquetball, and I can swim well enough to stay afloat, at least, and I drive a car much better than most if I do say so myself. My car has modified foot pedals. For steering and shifting, though, I get along fine with the standard hand controls. New passengers tend to look anxious at first; then, after we've gone a few miles, they forget all about it.

I daydream of switching to standard pedals, but the Motor Vehicle people have these absurd regulations.

It occurred to me at the beginning that Dorothy might have come back on some special assignment. She'd been permitted to return just long enough to tell me something, perhaps, after which she would be on her way. (I have to say right now that *who* had permitted her was not something I cared to dwell on. I am an atheist. Having her here in the first place had already shaken up more preconceptions than I could easily absorb.)

You would think that I would be eager to know what this assignment was. But remember the corollary: once she'd completed it, she would leave. And I didn't think I could bear that.

So I adopted a sort of Zen approach. I lived in the moment. Dorothy appeared; I was at peace. I didn't ask questions, didn't probe, didn't study the whys and wherefores; I just took comfort in being with her. If she had started to say something that sounded, oh, message-like, I would have tried my best to deflect her; but she didn't. It seemed that she was living in the moment also. Then she would vanish again, but she wasn't really gone for good. I somehow knew that. I would wait, still as a pond, until she reappeared.

Once, she asked me, "How are things at Nandina's? Does she fret over you, and tut-tut?"

"Yes, well, you remember what she's like," I said.

I was silent a moment. Then I said, "You needed to ask? Somehow, I figured you would just know."

"Oh, no. I don't know anything at all," Dorothy said.

It seemed to me that there was a sadness in her voice, but then she smiled at me, so I supposed I'd just imagined it.

My mother felt, to the end of her days, that my differences were her fault. She should have called the pediatrician earlier in my illness. She should have rushed me to the emergency room; forget the pediatrician. "They would only have sent us home again," I told her. "They'd have said that some virus was going around; just give me fluids and bed rest."

"I would have sat smack down on the floor and told them we weren't leaving," she said.

"Oh, why make such a big deal about it? I manage perfectly well."

"*Manage.* Yes, I suppose you do," she said. "And I wouldn't give it another thought if you had been lame from birth. But you weren't. You're not the way you started out. You're not who you were meant to be."

"Maybe this is *exactly* who I was meant to be," I said.

She just sighed. I was never going to understand.

"Anyhow," I said, "you did call the pediatrician. You told me. You called as soon as my fever went up."

"That man was an imbecile," she said, off on another tack. "He claimed fevers were nature's cure-all. He claimed they didn't do half as much harm as all those hysterical mothers dunking their children in ice water."

"Mom. Get over it," I said.

But she never did.

She was a homemaker (as she termed it), from the last generation of women who married straight out of college. She graduated in June of 1958 and married in July. Then had to wait ten years for her first baby, poor woman, but even so she didn't get a job. How did she fill that time, I wonder? Nandina and I were her entire occupation, once we came along. She built our science projects with us, and our dioramas. She ironed our underwear. She decorated our rooms in little-girl style and little-boy style—rosebuds for Nandina and sports banners for me. Never mind that Nandina was not the rosebud type, or that any time I took part in a sport my mother had apoplexy.

I was a rough-and-ready kind of kid, despite my differences.

I was clumsy but enthusiastic, eager to join whatever pickup game was happening on our block. Mom would literally wring her hands as she watched from the front window, but my father told her to let me do whatever I felt capable of. He wasn't as much of a worrier. But of course he was off at the office all day, and middle-aged by then besides. He was never the kind of father I could toss a football with on weekends, or ask to coach my Little League team.

So I mostly spent my childhood fending off the two women in my life—my mother and my sister, both of them lying in wait to cosset me to death. Even that young, I sensed the danger. You get sucked in. You turn soft. They have you where they want you then.

Is it any wonder I found Dorothy a breath of fresh air?

The first time she saw me, she said, "What's wrong with your arm?" She was wearing her white coat and she asked in a brusque, clinical tone. When I explained, she just said, "Huh," and went on to another subject.

The first time she rode in my car, she didn't so much as glance over, not even at the very start, to check how I was driving. She was too busy huffing on her glasses and polishing them with her sleeve.

And the first time she heard me stammer (after I fell in love with her and grew flustery and awkward), she cocked her head and said, "What is *that*? The brain injury, or just nerves?"

"Oh, just—just—nerves," I said.

"Really? I wonder," she said. "When you're dealing with the left hemisphere . . . Damn."

"Excuse me?"

"I think I left my keys in my office," she said.

.   .   .

She was unique among women, Dorothy. She was one of a kind. Lord, she left a hole behind. I felt as if I'd been erased, as if I'd been ripped in two.

Then I looked down the street and saw her standing on the sidewalk.

2

Here is how she died.

It was August. Early August of 2007, oppressively hot and muggy. I happened to have a cold. Summer is the very worst time for a cold, I always think. You can't just pile on the blankets and sweat it out the way you would in winter. You're already sweating, only not in any way that's beneficial.

I went in to work as usual, but the air conditioning made my teeth start chattering as soon as I got settled. I hunched over my desk shivering and shaking, sneezing and coughing and blowing my nose and heaping used tissues in my wastebasket, till Irene ordered me home. That was Irene for you. She claimed I was contaminating the office. The others—Nandina and the rest—had been urging me to leave for my own sake. "You look miserable, poor thing," our secretary said. But Irene took a more self-centered approach. "I refuse to sacrifice my health to your misguided work ethic," she told me.

So I said, "Fine. I'll go." Since she put it *that* way.

Nandina said, "Shall I drive you?" but I said, "I'm still able to function, thank you very much." Then I gathered my things and stalked out, mad at all of them and madder still at myself, for falling ill in the first place. I hate to look like an invalid.

Alone in the car, though, I allowed myself some moaning and groaning. I sneezed and gave a long-drawn-out "Aaah," as if I were a good deal sicker than I was. I glanced in the rearview mirror and saw that my eyes were streaming with tears. My face was flushed and my hair had a damp and matted look.

We lived just off Cold Spring Lane, in an unkempt, wooded area a few minutes' drive from downtown. Our house was a little white bungalow. Not what you would call fancy, but, then, neither Dorothy nor I was the *Better Homes and Gardens* type. The place suited us just fine: all on one floor, with a light-filled sunporch tacked onto the living room where we could stash the computer and Dorothy's medical journals.

It was my intention to proceed directly to the sunporch and get some work done. I had brought a manuscript home with me for editing. Halfway through the living room, though, I found myself making a detour to the sofa. I sank onto it and groaned again, and then I let my papers drop to the floor and stretched out full-length.

But you know how a cold reacts to a horizontal position. Immediately, I stopped being able to breathe. My head felt like a cannonball. I was hoping to sleep, but I seemed to be filled all at once with a brittle, edgy alertness. I found the normal clutter of our living room intensely irritating—the apple core browning on the coffee table, the unsorted laundry heaped in an armchair, the newspapers on the sofa interfering with the placement of my feet. One part of my mind grew suddenly ambitious, and I imagined springing up and whipping things into shape. Dragging out the vacuum cleaner, even. Doing something about that stain on the carpet in front of the fireplace. My body went on lying there, dull and achy, while my mind performed over and over the same frenetic chores. It was exhausting.

Time must have passed somehow or other, though, because when the doorbell rang, I checked my watch and found that it was past noon. I got up with a sigh and went out to the front hall to open the door. Our secretary was standing there with a grocery bag on her hip. "Feeling any better?" she asked me.

"Oh, yes."

"Well, I've brought you some soup," she said. "We all just knew you wouldn't be fixing yourself any lunch."

"Thanks, but I'm not—"

"Feed a cold, starve a fever!" she caroled. She nudged the door wider open with her elbow and stepped inside. "People always wonder which it is," she said. "'Feed a cold and starve a fever,' or 'Starve a cold and feed a fever.' But what they don't realize is, it's an 'If, then' construction. So in that case either one will work, because *if* you feed a cold *then* you'll be starving a fever, which you most certainly do want to do, and if you starve a cold then you'll be feeding a nasty old fever."

By now, she was walking right past me down the hall—one of those women who feel sure they know what's best for you in all situations. Not unlike my sister, in fact. Except where Nandina was long and gawky, Peggy was soft and dimpled—a pink-and-gold person with a cloud of airy blond curls and a fondness for thrift-store outfits involving too many bits of lace. I liked Peggy just fine (we'd gone through grade school together, which may have been what led my father to hire her), but the softness was misleading. She held our entire office together; she was way, way more than a secretary. Any time she took a day off, the rest of us fell apart—couldn't even find the stapler. Now she headed unerringly toward the kitchen, pad-pad in her Chinese silk slippers, although as far as I could recall she had never been in our kitchen. I trailed after her, saying, "Really, I'm not hungry. I'm *really* not hungry. All I want to do is—"

"Just a little soup?" she asked. "Cream of tomato? Chicken noodle?"

"Neither."

"Deether," it sounded like. I could have been in a nose-spray commercial.

She said, "The cream of tomato was Nandina's idea, but I thought chicken noodle for protein."

"Deether!" I told her.

"Okay, then, just tea. My special magic tea for sore throats."

She set the grocery bag on the counter and pulled out a box of Constant Comment. "I brought decaf," she said, "so it won't interfere with your sleep. Because sleep, you know, is the very best cure-all." Next came a lemon and a bottle of honey. "You should get back on the couch."

"But I don't—"

"Don't" was "dote." Peggy heard, finally. She turned from the sink, where she'd started filling the kettle. "*Listen* to you!" she said. "Should I phone Dorothy?"

"No!" Doe.

"I could just leave a message with her office. I wouldn't have to interrupt her."

"Doe."

"Well, suit yourself," she said, and she set the kettle on the burner. Our stove was so old-fashioned that you had to light it by hand, which she somehow knew ahead of time, because she reached for the matchbox without even seeming to look for it. I sat down on one of the kitchen chairs. I watched her slice the lemon in half and squeeze it into a mug while she discussed the proven powers of fruit pectin in bolstering the immune system. "That's why the Constant Comment," she said, "on account of the orange peels in it," and then she said that when *she* got a cold, which wasn't all that often because somehow she just seemed to have this natural, inborn resistance to colds . . .

Talk about Constant Comment.

She poured a huge amount of honey on top of the lemon. I swear she poured a quarter of a cup. I didn't see how there'd be any room for the water. Then she plopped in two teabags, draping the strings over the rim of the mug with her little finger prinked out in a lady-of-the-manor style that must have been meant as a joke, because next she said, in a fake English accent, "This will be veddy, veddy tasty, old chap."

I realized all at once that I had a really bad headache, and I was fairly certain that I hadn't had it before she got there.

While we waited for the tea to steep, she went off to fetch an afghan. We didn't own an afghan, to the best of my knowledge, but I failed to tell her so because I welcomed the peace and quiet. Then she came back, still talking. She said when her father had had a cold he used to eat an onion. "Ate it raw," she said, "like an apple." She was carrying an afghan made of stitched-together hexagons. Possibly she had found it in the linen closet off our bedroom, and I knew we'd left the bedroom a mess. Well, that was what people had to expect when they barged in uninvited. She draped the afghan around my shoulders and tucked it under my chin as if I were a two-year-old, while I shrank inward as much as possible. "Once, when my mom had a cold, Daddy got *her* to eat an onion," she said. "She instantly threw it up again, though." My ears were a little clogged, and her voice had a muffled, distant sound like something you'd hear in a dream.

But the tea, when it was ready, did soothe my throat. The vapors helped my breathing some, too. I drank it in slow sips, huddled under my afghan. Peggy said that, in her opinion, her father should have cooked the onion. "Maybe simmered it with honey," she said, "because you know how honey has antibacterial properties." She was wiping all the counters now. I didn't try to stop her. What good would it have done? I polished off the last of the tea—the dregs tooth-achingly sweet—and then without a word I set down the mug and went back to the living room. The afghan trailed behind me with a ssh-ing sound, picking up stray bits of lint and crumbs along the way. I collapsed on the sofa. I curled up in a fetal position so as to avoid the newspapers, and I fell into a deep sleep.

When I woke, the front door was opening. I figured Peggy was leaving. But then I heard the jingle of keys landing in the porcelain bowl in the hall. I called, "Dorothy?"

"Hmm?"

She came through the archway reading something, a postcard she must have found on the floor beneath the mail slot. When she glanced up, she said, "Oh. Are you sick?"

"Just a little sniffly." I struggled to a sitting position and looked at my watch. "It's five o'clock!"

She misunderstood; she said, "I had a cancellation."

"I've been asleep all afternoon!"

"You didn't go in to work?" she asked.

"I did, but Irene sent me home."

Dorothy gave a snort of amusement. (She knew how Irene could be.)

"And then Peggy stopped by with soup."

Another snort; she knew Peggy, too. She tossed the mail on the coffee table and removed her satchel from her shoulder. Dorothy didn't hold with purses. She carried her satchel everywhere—a scuffed brown leather affair with the bellows stretched to the breaking point, the kind that belonged to spies in old black-and-white movies. Her doctor coat, which she was shrugging off now, had a dingy diagonal mark across the chest from the strap. People often mistook Dorothy for some sort of restaurant employee—and not the head chef, either. Sometimes I found that amusing, although other times I didn't.

When she went out to the kitchen, I knew she would be getting her Triscuits. That was what she had for her snack at the end of every workday: six Triscuits exactly, because six was the "serving size" listed on the box. She showed a slavish devotion to the concept of a recommended serving size, even when it was half a cupcake (which was more often the case than you might suppose).

Except that the Triscuits were missing, that day. She called from the kitchen, "Have you seen the Triscuits?"

"What? No," I said. I had swung my feet to the floor and was folding the afghan.

"I can't find them. They're not on the counter."

I said nothing, since I had no answer. A moment later, she

appeared in the dining-room doorway. "Did you clean up out there?" she asked.

"Who, me?"

"There's nothing on the counters at all. I can't find anything."

I grimaced and said, "That would be Peggy's doing, I guess."

"I wish she'd left well enough alone. Where could she have put the Triscuits?"

"I have no idea."

"I looked in the cupboards, I looked in the pantry . . ."

"I'm sure they'll show up by and by," I said.

"But what'll I eat in the meantime?"

"Wheat Thins?" I suggested.

"I don't like Wheat Thins," Dorothy said. "I like Triscuits."

I tipped my head back against the sofa. I was getting a little tired of the subject, to be honest.

Unfortunately, she noticed. "This may not be important to *you*," she said, "but I haven't had a thing to eat all day. All I've had is coffee! I'm famished."

"Well, whose fault is that?" I asked her. (We'd been through this discussion before.)

"You know I'm too busy to eat."

"Dorothy," I said. "From the time you wake up in the morning till the time you get home in the evening, you're living on coffee and sugar and cream. Mostly sugar and cream. And you call yourself a doctor!"

"I *am* a doctor," she said. "A very hardworking doctor. I don't have any free time."

"Neither does the rest of the world, but somehow they manage to fit in a meal now and then."

"Well, maybe the rest of the world is not so conscientious," she said.

She had her fists on her hips now. She looked a little bit like a bulldog. I'd never realized that before.

Oh, why, why, why did I have to realize on that particular afternoon? Why could I not have said, "Look. Clearly you're half starved, and it seems to be making you fractious. Let's go out to the kitchen and find you something to eat"?

I'll tell you why: it's because next she said, "But what would *you* know about it? You with your nursemaids rushing around brewing your homemade soup."

"It wasn't homemade; it was canned," I said. "And I didn't *ask* for soup. I didn't even eat it. I told Peggy I didn't want it."

"How come she was in the kitchen, then?"

"She was making me some tea."

"Tea!" Dorothy echoed. I might as well have said opium. "She made you *tea*?"

"What's wrong with that?"

"You don't even like tea!"

"This was medicinal tea, for my throat."

"Oh, for your *throat*," Dorothy said, with exaggerated sympathy.

"I had a sore throat, Dorothy."

"An ordinary sore throat, and everyone comes running. Why does that always happen? Throngs of devoted attendants falling all over themselves to take care of you."

"Well, some—some—somebody had to do it," I said. "I don't see *you* taking care of me."

Dorothy was quiet a moment. Then she dropped her fists

from her hips and walked over to her satchel. She picked it up and went into the sunporch. I heard the leathery creak as she set her satchel on the desk, and then the squeak of the swivel chair.

Stupid argument. We had them, now and then. What couple doesn't? We weren't living in a fairy tale. Still, this particular argument seemed unusually pointless. In actual fact I hated being taken care of, and had deliberately chosen a non-caretaker for my wife. And Dorothy wouldn't mind at all if somebody made me tea. Most likely she'd be relieved. This was just one of those silly spats about something neither one of us gave a damn about, but now we were backed in our corners and didn't know how to get out of them.

I heaved myself from the sofa and crossed the hall to the bedroom. I closed the door soundlessly and sat down on the edge of the bed, where I took off my shoes and my brace. (I wear a polypropylene brace to correct a foot-drop.) The Velcro straps made a ripping sound as I undid them—*batch! batch!*—and I winced, because I didn't want Dorothy guessing what I was up to. I wanted her to wonder, a little bit.

I held still and listened for her, but all I heard was another creak. This would not have been her satchel, though. She was too far away for that. It was probably a hall floorboard, I decided.

I stretched out on the rumpled sheets and stared at the ceiling. There wasn't a chance on earth I could sleep. I realized that now. I had slept all afternoon. What I should do was go out to the kitchen and start cooking something good-smelling, something that would lure Dorothy from the sunporch. How about hamburgers? I knew we had a pound of—

Creak! An even louder one. Or not a creak after all, but a crash, because the creak lasted too long and then it swelled into a *slam!* with smaller slams following it, and stray tinkles and crackles and thumps. My first thought (I know this was ludicrous) was that Dorothy must be much more miffed than I had supposed. But even as I was thinking it, I had to admit that she was not the type to throw tantrums. I sat straight up and my heart began hammering. I called, "Dorothy?" I stumbled off the bed. "Dorothy! What was that?"

I made it to the door in my stocking feet, and then I remembered my brace. I could walk without it, in a fashion, but it would be slow going. Turn back and strap it on? No; no time for that. And where had I put my cane? That was anybody's guess. I flung open the bedroom door.

It seemed I was on the edge of a forest.

The hall was a mass of twigs and leaves and bits of bark. Even the air was filled with bark—dry bark chips floating in a dusty haze, and a small bird or a very large insect suddenly whizzing up out of nowhere. Isolated pings! and ticks! and pops! rang out as different objects settled—a pane of glass falling from a window, something wooden landing on the wooden floor. I grabbed on to a broken-off branch and used it for support as I worked my way around it. It wasn't clear to me yet what had happened. I was in a daze, maybe even in shock, and there was a lag in my comprehension. All I knew was that this forest was thicker in the living room, and that Dorothy was beyond that, in the sunporch, where I could see nothing but leaves, leaves, leaves, and branches as thick as my torso.

"*Dorothy!*"

No answer.

I was standing near the coffee table. I could make out one corner of it, the egg-and-dart molding around the rim, and wasn't it interesting that the phrase "egg-and-dart" should come to me so handily. I looked toward the sunporch again and saw that I could never fight my way through that jungle, so I turned back, planning to go out the front door and around to the side of the house, to the outside entrance of the sunporch. On my way toward the hall, though, I passed the lamp table next to the sofa (the sofa invisible now), where the cordless telephone lay, littered with more bits of bark. I picked it up and pressed *Talk*. Miraculously, I heard a dial tone. I tried to punch in 911, but my hand was shaking so that I kept hitting the pound sign by accident. I had to redial twice before I finally connected. I put the phone to my ear.

A woman said, "Please file an ambulance."

"What?"

"Please file an ambulance."

"What?"

"Police?" she said in a weary tone. "Fire? Or ambulance."

"Oh, pol—pol—or—I don't know! Fire! No, ambulance! Ambulance!"

"What is the problem, sir," she said.

"A t-t-t-tree fell!" I said, and that was the first moment when I seemed to understand what had happened. "A tree fell on my house!"

She took down my information so slowly that her slowness seemed meant to be instructive, an example of how to behave. But I had things to do! I couldn't stand here all day! I had read that 911 operators could detect a caller's address with special equipment, and I failed to see why she was asking me all these questions she must already know the answers to. I said, "I have to go! I have to go!" which reminded me, absurdly, of a child needing to pee, and all at once it seemed to me that I did need to pee, and I wondered how long it would be before I could attend again to such a mundane task.

I heard a siren from far away. I still don't know if it was my phone call that brought it. In any case, I dropped the phone without saying goodbye and staggered toward the hall.

When I opened the front door, I found more tree outside. I had somehow expected that once I left the house I would be free and clear. I batted away branches, spat out gnats and grit. The siren was so loud that it felt like a knife in my ears. Then it stopped, and I saw the fire truck as I stepped out from the last of the tree: a beautiful, shiny red, with an ambulance pulling up behind it. A man in full firefighting regalia—but why?—jumped down from the truck and shouted, "Don't move! Stay there! They'll bring a stretcher!"

I kept walking, because how would they know where to bring it if I didn't show them? "Stop!" he shouted, and an ambulance man—*not* with a stretcher; no sign of a stretcher—ran up and wrapped his arms around me like a straitjacket. "Wait here. Don't try to walk," he said. His breath smelled of chili.

"I can walk fine," I told him.

"J.B.! Bring the stretcher!"

They thought I was the one who was injured, I guess. I mean, recently injured. I fought him off. I said, "My wife! Around—around—around—"

"All right, buddy. Calm down."

"Where is she?" a fireman asked.

"Around the—"

I waved my arm. Then I turned toward where I was waving—the north side of the house—and found that it no longer existed. All I saw was tree and more tree.

The fireman said, "*Oh,* man."

I knew that tree. It was a white oak. It had stood in our backyard forever, probably since long before our house was built, and it was enormous, a good foot and a half in diameter at the base, with such a pronounced tilt in the direction of our roof that I had it inspected every September, when the tree men came to prune. But they always assured me it was healthy. Old, yes, and perhaps not putting out quite as many leaves as it used to, but healthy. "And besides," the foreman had told me, "if it ever *was* to fall, it's standing so close to the house that it wouldn't do much damage. It would only, more like, *lean onto* the house. It doesn't have enough room to gather any speed."

But he had been wrong. First of all, the tree had obviously not been healthy. It had fallen on a day without a breath of wind, without so much as a breeze. And second, it had done a *lot* of damage. It had leaned at the start, granted (that must have been the first creak I heard), but then it went on to buckle the roof from the center all the way to one end. And it had smashed the sunporch absolutely flat.

I said, "Get her out! Get her out! Get her out!"

The man who was holding me said, "Okay, brother, hang on." By now he was holding me *up,* really. Somehow my knees had given way. He backed me toward a wrought-iron lawn chair that we never sat in and helped me sit. "Any pain?" he asked me, and I said, "No! Get her out!"

I wished I did have pain. I *hated* my body. I hated sitting there like a dummy while stronger, abler men fought to rescue my wife.

They called for work crews and chain saws and axes, and police cars to block off the street and a crane to raise the largest section of the tree trunk. They shouted over their radios and they crackled through the branches. This all must have taken some time, but I can't tell you how much. Meanwhile, a crowd had gathered, our neighbors and stray passersby. Old Mimi King from across the alley brought me a glass of iced tea. (I took a token sip, to be nice.) Jim Rust laid a pink knit crib blanket over my shoulders. It must have been eighty-some degrees and I was streaming sweat, but I thanked him. "She's going to be *just fine*," I told him, because he hadn't said it himself, and I thought somebody ought to.

He said, "I certainly hope so, Aaron."

It bothered me that he spoke my name like that. I was the only person listening. He didn't need to specify whom he was addressing, for God's sake.

Two men staggered out of the branches with a big heavy pile of old clothes. They laid the pile on a stretcher and my heart lurched. I said, "What—?" I struggled up from my chair and nearly crumpled to the ground. I grabbed on to Jim for support. He called out to them, "Is she alive?" and I thought, *He has no business! That's MY question to ask!* But a fireman said, "She's got a pulse," and then I felt so grateful to Jim that tears came to my eyes. I clutched his arm tighter and said, "Take me—take—" and he understood and led me closer.

Her face was the same moon shape, round-cheeked and smooth, eyes closed, but she was filthy dirty. And the mound of her bosom was more of a . . . cave. But that was understandable! She was lying on her back! You know how a woman's breasts go flat when she's lying on her . . .

"At least there's no blood," I told Jim. "I don't see a bit of blood."

"No, Aaron," he said.

I wished he'd stop saying my name.

I wanted to ride with her in the ambulance, but too many people were working on her. They told me to meet them at the hospital instead. By that time we had been joined by Jim's wife, Mary-Clyde, and she said she and Jim would drive me. Mary-Clyde was a schoolteacher, full of crisp authority. When I told her I could drive myself, she said, "Of course you can, but then you'd have to park and such, so we'll just do it this way, shall we." I said, meekly, "Okay." Then she asked where she could find my shoes. Jim said, "Oh, Mary-Clyde, he doesn't care about his shoes at a time like this." But in fact I did care; I'm sorry, but I did; and I told her where they were and asked her to bring my brace as well.

They took Dorothy to Johns Hopkins. Hopkins was the very highest-tech, the most advanced and cutting-edge, so that was good. But on the other hand, it was the place that any Baltimorean with a grain of sense knew to avoid except in the direst circumstances—a gigantic, unfeeling, Dickensian labyrinth where patients could languish forgotten for hours in peeling basement corridors, and so that was very bad. Oh, welcome to the world of the Next of Kin: good news, bad news, up, down, up, and down again, over days that lasted forever. The surgery was successful but then it was not, and she had to be rushed back to the operating room. She was "stabilized," whatever that meant, but then all her machines went crazy. It got so, every time a doctor peeked into the waiting room, I would ostentatiously look in the other direction, like a prisoner trying to pretend that my torturer couldn't faze me. Other people—the strangers camped in their own cozy groups all around me—glanced up eagerly, but not me.

I was allowed to see her just briefly, at wide intervals. I don't know that you could really call it *seeing* her, though. Her face was completely obscured by tubes and cords and hoses. One hand lay outside the sheet, one of her chubby tan hands with the darker knuckles, but it was punctured by another tube and thickly adhesive-taped, so that I couldn't hold it. And her fingers were flaccid, like clay. It was obvious that she wouldn't have been aware of my touch, in any event.

"Guess what, Dorothy," I said to her motionless form. "You know that oak tree I used to worry about?"

There was so much I wanted to tell her. Not just about the oak tree; forget the oak tree. I don't know why I even mentioned the oak tree. I wanted to say, "Dorothy, if I could press *Rewind* right now and send us back to our little house, I would never shut myself away in a separate room. I would follow you into the sunporch. I would come up behind where you were sitting at your desk and lay my cheek on top of your warm head till you turned around."

She would have given one of her snorts if she had heard that.

I would have snorted myself, once upon a time.

Here is something funny: I'd lost my cold. I don't mean I got over it; I mean it just disappeared, at some point between when I drank that tea and when I walked into the waiting room. I'm guessing it was while they were trying to rescue Dorothy. I remember sitting under Jim Rust's pink blanket, and I wasn't sneezing then or blowing my nose. Maybe a cold could be shaken out of a person by the slam of a tree trunk, or by psychic trauma. Or a combination of the two.

They kept urging me to go home for a spell and get some rest. Go to Nandina's, was what they meant, since everybody felt my own house was uninhabitable. Jim and Mary-Clyde urged it, and all the people from work, and various stray acquaintances. (My oak tree had been mentioned in the paper, evidently.) They came with their wrapped sandwiches and their covered containers of salad that I couldn't bear to look at, let alone eat; even Irene arrived with a box of gourmet chocolates; and they promised to hold down the fort while I grabbed a little break. But I refused to leave. I suspect I may have thought I was keeping Dorothy alive somehow. (Don't laugh.) I didn't even go home to change. I stayed in my same dingy clothes, and my face grew stubbled and itchy.

After Mary-Clyde located my cane, though, I did start taking brief walks up and down the corridor. This was not because I wanted to, but because my leg had started seizing up from lack of use. I fell down once, when I was heading toward the restroom. So I would choose a time just after my allotted few minutes with Dorothy, and I would let the staff know exactly where I would be and when I was coming back. "Fine," they would say, hardly listening. I would go into a flurry of parting instructions—"You might want to check if she's warm enough; I've been thinking she's not quite—"

"Yes, we'll see to it; run along."

What I really wanted to say was, "This is a specific person, do you understand? Not just some *patient*. I want to make sure you realize that."

"Mmhmm," they'd have murmured.

I walked up and down the corridors with a sense of something stretching thin, fragile elastic threads stretching between me and Dorothy, and I saw sights I tried to forget. I saw huge-eyed children without any hair, and skeletal men struggling for breath, and old people lying on gurneys with so many bags and tubes attached that they'd stopped being human beings. I looked away. I couldn't look. I turned and went back to my torturers.

The shoes arrived in front of me on a Wednesday afternoon. I knew it was a Wednesday because the newspaper on the chair beside mine had a color photo of a disgusting seafood lasagna. (Wednesday always seems to be food day, for newspapers.) The shoes were clogs. Black leather clogs. That's what the hospital staff tended to wear, I'd observed. Very unprofessional-looking. I raised my eyes. It was a male nurse; I knew him. Or recognized him, I mean. From other occasions. He'd been one of the kind ones. He said, "Mr. Woolcott?"

"Yes."

"Why don't you come with me."

I stood up and reached for my cane. I followed him through the door and into the ICU. It wasn't time for a visit yet. I had just had my visit, not half an hour before. I felt singled out and privileged, but then also a little, I don't know, apprehensive.

The cords and hoses had been removed and she lay uncannily still. I had thought she was still before, but I had had no idea. I had been so ignorant.

3

There used to be a dairy outlet over on Reisterstown Road, with a lighted white glass sign outside reading FIRST WITH THE CARRIAGE TRADE. It showed the silhouette of a woman wheeling a baby carriage—a witticism, I guess—and she was just *galloping* along, taking huge confident strides in a dress that flared below her knees although we were in the era of miniskirts. Whenever my family drove past that sign, I thought of my sister. This was before my sister had reached her teens, even, but still I thought of her, for Nandina seemed to have been born lanky, and ungainly, and lacking in all fashion sense. I'm not saying she was unattractive. She had clear gray eyes, and excellent skin, and shiny brown hair that she wore pulled straight back from her forehead with a single silver barrette. But the barrette tells you everything: she wore it still, although she would be forty on her next birthday. An aging girl, was what she was, and had been from earliest childhood. Her shoes were Mary Janes, as flat as scows in order to minimize her height. Her elbows jutted like coat hangers, and her legs descended as straight as reeds to her Ping-Pong-ball anklebones.

She drove me home from the hospital the afternoon that Dorothy died, and I sat beside her envying her imperviousness. She kept both hands on the steering wheel at the ten and two o'clock positions, just as our father had taught her all those years ago. Her posture was impeccable. (She had never been one of those women who imagine that slouching makes them look shorter.) At first she attempted some small talk—hot day, no rain in the forecast, pity the poor farmers—but when she saw that I wasn't up to it, she stopped. That was one good thing about Nandina. She wasn't bothered by silence.

We were traveling through the blasted wasteland surrounding Hopkins, with its boarded-up row houses and trash-littered sidewalks, but what struck me was how healthy everyone was. That woman yanking her toddler by the wrist, those teenagers shoving each other off the curb, that man peering stealthily into a parked car: there was nothing physically wrong with them. A boy standing at an intersection had so much excess energy that he bounced from foot to foot as he waited for us to pass. People looked so robust, so indestructible.

I pivoted to peer out the rear window at Hopkins, its antique dome and lofty pedestrian bridges and flanks of tall buildings—an entire complex city rising in the distance like some kind of Camelot. Then I faced forward again.

Nandina wanted to take me to her house. She thought mine wasn't fit to live in. But I was clinging to the notion of being on my own, finally, free from all those pitying looks and sympathetic murmurs, and I insisted on her driving me home. It should have tipped me off that she gave in so readily. Turns out she was figuring I would change my mind once I got there. As soon as we reached my block she slowed down, the better to let me absorb the effect of the twigs and small branches carpeting the whole street—*my* twigs and small branches. She drew to a stop in front of my house and switched off the ignition. "Why don't I just wait," she said, "till you make sure you're going to feel comfortable here."

For a minute I didn't answer. I was staring at the house. It was true that it was in even worse shape than I had pictured. The fallen tree lay everywhere, not in a single straight line but flung all across the yard as if it had shattered on impact. The whole northern end of the house slumped toward the ground, nearly flattening as it reached the sunporch. Most of the roof was covered with a sheet of bright-blue plastic. Jim Rust had arranged for that. I vaguely remembered his telling me about it. The plastic dipped at the ridgepole in a way that reminded me of the dip in Dorothy's chest when the rescuers carried her out, but never mind; don't think about that; think about something else. I turned to Nandina and said, "I'll be fine. Thanks for the lift."

"Maybe I should come in with you."

"Nandina. Go."

She sighed and switched the ignition back on. I gave her a peck on the cheek—a concession. (I'm not usually so demonstrative.) Then I heaved myself out of the car and shut the door and strode off.

It took a moment before I heard her drive away, but she did, finally.

Just in case some of the neighbors were watching from their windows, I made a point of approaching the house like any other man heading home after an outing. I stabbed the front sidewalk briskly with my cane; I glanced around at the fallen branches with mild interest. I unlocked my front door, opened it, shut it behind me. Sagged back against it as if I'd been kicked in the stomach.

An eerie blue light filled the hall, from the blue tarp overhead that showed through the gaps in the ceiling. The living room was too much of a jungle to navigate, and of course I didn't even try to look beyond it to the sunporch. I stepped across a floorful of mail and made my way to the rear of the house. In the kitchen I was relieved to find only a scattering of wood chips on every surface, and one broken windowpane where a stray twig had poked through. But the dining room, to the right, was a ruin. I closed the door again after the briefest glance inside. That was okay, though. A person could live just fine without a dining room! I could eat in the kitchen. I went over to the sink and turned the faucet on. Water flowed immediately.

In the bottom of the sink sat a mug, the interior glazed with dried honey and stippled with bark dust, a teaspoon slanting out of it.

Sometimes the most recent moments can seem so long, long ago.

I walked back through the hall to check the guest room, the bathroom, and our bedroom. All fine. Maybe I could turn the guest room into a makeshift living room while I was having repairs done. In the shower stall I found a grasshopper. I let it stay where it was. In the bedroom I was tempted to lie down and simply crash—not so much sleep as tumble into unconsciousness— but I didn't give in. I had an assignment to complete. I went to Dorothy's side of the bed and pulled open the drawer of her nightstand. My fear was that she had taken her address book to the sunporch, which sometimes happened; but no, there it lay, underneath an issue of *Radiology Management*.

Her family's name was Rosales. (It was her name, too. She hadn't changed it when we married.) There were several Rosaleses in the address book, all written in Dorothy's jagged, awkward hand, but the one I settled on was Tyrone, her oldest brother. He'd become head of the family after her father died, and I figured that if I phoned him I wouldn't have to phone the others. I also figured that, with luck, I might get Tyrone's wife instead, since in Texas it was barely past midday and Tyrone himself would most likely be at work. I had never met Tyrone or his wife, either one—or anybody else in the family, for that matter—but it seemed to me that a mere sister-in-law would be less subject to some sort of emotional reaction. I was very concerned about the possibility of an emotional reaction. Really I didn't want to make this call at all. Couldn't we just go on as if nothing had happened, since Dorothy never saw her family anyhow? Who would be the wiser? But Nandina had told me I had to do it.

The phone at the other end rang three times, which was long enough for me to start hoping for an answering machine. (Although I knew full well that it would be wrong to leave a mere message.) Then a sharp click. "Hello?" A man's voice, low and growly.

"Tyrone Rosales?"

"Who's this?"

"This is—this is—"

Of all times, of all impermissible times, I was going to have my speech problem. I made myself go quiet. I took a deep breath. "Aaron," I said very slowly. I have more success with *A* words, as long as I slide into them without any hard-edged beginning.

"Woolcott" felt as if it might present difficulties, though, so I said, "Your b-b-broth—"

"Aaron, *Dorothy's* husband?" he asked.

"Mmhmm."

"What's up?"

I took another breath.

"Is something wrong with her?" he asked.

I said, "A t-t-t—a tree fell on the house."

Silence.

"A tree fell on the house," I said again.

"Is she okay?"

I said, "No."

"Is she dead?"

I said, "Yes."

"Oh," Tyrone said. "Good God."

I waited for him to absorb it. Besides, it felt restful, not talking. Finally he said, "When's the service?"

"There won't—won't—no service."

Nandina and I had already decided. And no burial, either; just cremation. I thought Dorothy would prefer that.

Tyrone said, "No service."

A pause.

"She was raised religious," he said.

"Yes, but—"

It seemed best to leave it at that: Yes, but.

"Well," Tyrone said after a minute, "anyhow, it wouldn't've been so easy for us to leave the animals."

"Right."

"Did she suffer?"

"No!"

I took another breath.

"No," I said, "she did not suffer."

"She always was real spunky. Real mind of her own."

"It's true."

"I remember once, when we were kids, me and the others were chewing soft tar from the road on this really hot day and Dorothy comes along and we say, 'Here, Dorothy, try some.' She says, 'Are you kidding?' Says, 'Why would I want to eat a *highway*?'"

That sounded like Dorothy, all right. I could hear her saying it. Dorothy as a child had always seemed unimaginable, but now I could imagine her clearly.

"She was named for the girl in *The Wizard of Oz*," Tyrone said. "I guess she mentioned that."

"Oh. No, she didn't."

"That was our grandpa's idea. He was the one who named all of us. He wanted to make sure we sounded American."

"I see."

"So," he said. "Anyhow. Thanks for the phone call. Sorry for your loss."

"I'm sorry for *your* loss," I told him.

After that, there was nothing more for us to say. Although I felt this odd reluctance to let him hang up. For a while there, while he was talking, Dorothy had been her old self again: strong-willed and sturdy and stubborn. Not the passive victim she had become in her final days.

It was a good thing I had a job to go to. My job was my salvation. I went in early, took no breaks, didn't stop for lunch. The only drawback was my co-workers, so long-faced and solicitous. Well, except for Irene. Nobody would ever accuse Irene of solicitude. But I was avoiding Irene, because, I don't know, I guess over the years I'd had a little crush on her, and now that seemed obscene. All at once I didn't even like her.

So I made sure to arrive before any of the others, and I'd hurry straight to my office and close the door behind me. Later I'd hear Nandina come in, or I could assume it was Nandina since she was our early bird as a rule. Then, after that, Charles and Peggy, and finally Irene. I'd hear murmurs in the outer room and laughter and the ringing of a phone. Eventually, Peggy would tap on my door with just the tips of her fingers. "Aaron? Are you in there?"

"Mmhmm."

"Coffee's made. Shall I bring you some?"

"No, thanks."

A hesitation. Then the sound of her soft-soled shoes padding away again.

It had never been my plan to go into the family business. I attended college at Stanford, on the other side of the continent, and I'd expected to remain out there and make my own way in the world. But my father had his first heart attack right about the time I graduated, and he asked me to come home and run things while he convalesced. Now that I look back, I see how I let myself be bamboozled. Nandina, it turned out, was running things just fine. I guess I just liked to think that someone needed me. Besides which, I'd had nothing more specific in mind, having majored in English.

In my great-grandfather's time the company called itself a "gentleman's publisher," which was their euphemism for "vanity press." Even now we were sort of mealy-mouthed about it, although the word "gentleman's" had been replaced in modern times by "private." Still, the principle was the same. The majority of our authors paid *us,* and most did not welcome my editing advice, although, believe me, they could have used it.

In fact, once those print-on-demand outfits started popping up on the Internet, I might very well have found myself out of a job if not for Charles. Charles was our sales rep, and he dreamed up, single-handedly, the concept of the *Beginner's* series. *The Beginner's Wine Guide, The Beginner's Monthly Budget, The Beginner's Book of Dog Training.* These were something on the order of the *Dummies* books, but without the cheerleader tone of voice—more dignified. And far more classily designed, with deckle-edged pages and uniform hard-backed bindings wrapped in expensive, glossy covers. Also, we were more focused— sometimes absurdly so, if you asked me. (Witness *The Beginner's Spice Cabinet.*) Anything is manageable if it's divided into small enough increments, was the theory; even life's most complicated lessons. Not *The Beginner's Cookbook* but *The Beginner's Soups, The Beginner's Desserts,* and *The Beginner's Dinner Party,* which led the reader through one perfect company meal from start to finish, including grocery list. Not *The Beginner's Child Care* but *The Beginner's Colicky Baby*—our best-seller, in its modest way, and continually in print since the day it first appeared.

I was in sole charge of editing these, and Irene oversaw the design—even if she did call them "giftie books." Then Charles ran around marketing them like a man possessed. He was convinced that sooner or later the series would make us all rich, although so far it hadn't happened.

People often referred to us as The Beginner's Press, but that was most definitely not our name; good Lord, no. It would hardly have inspired confidence. We were Woolcott Publishing, the words spelled out in tall, slim, sans-serif lettering, all lower-case, considered very modern once upon a time. (But printed only on the front of the *Beginner's* books, of course, since the spines were far too narrow.)

In the first weeks after Dorothy died, I happened to be working on *The Beginner's Book of Birdwatching.* As usual, an expert had been employed to supply the raw material, an ornithologist from the University of Maryland, and the result was an incoherent overload of information that I was struggling to whip into shape—also as usual.

It was my practice to settle upon a mental image of one individual reader, the way public speakers are told to direct their words toward one individual listener. I had decided that our reader in this case was a young woman who had been invited to go birdwatching with a young man she secretly fancied. It would be their very first date. She would certainly not be expected to know the Latin names of the birds she saw (although my expert was chomping at the bit to provide them), but she needed help in her choices of what clothes to wear, what equipment to bring, and what questions to ask. Or should she stay totally silent? Predictably, my expert had not thought to address this issue. I phoned him for a consultation, several times over. I made hand-written notes in the margins. I crossed out, crossed out, crossed out. I was left with a book that was *too* slender, and I phoned him yet again.

At the end of every day I put everything away in my desk,

reached for my cane, rose to my feet, and approached my office door. There I squared my shoulders and assumed what I hoped was a cheerful, oblivious expression. Then I opened the door and strode out.

"Aaron! Calling it quits?"

"How're the birds going, Aaron?"

"Would you feel like coming home with me for a bite of supper?"

This last would be Nandina, who had her own private office, much bigger than mine, but somehow contrived, these days, to be standing in the outer room every evening as I walked through. "Oh," I'd tell her, "I guess I'll just head back to my place. But thanks." Peggy would be twisting a lace-edged handkerchief as she gazed at me. Charles would be staring fixedly at his computer, his face a mottled red with embarrassment. Irene would sit back in her chair with her head cocked, gauging the extent of the damage.

"Night, all!" I would say.

And out the heavy oak door and into the street, safe at last.

Back home, I'd find offerings of food waiting on my front stoop. I believe my neighbors had arranged some sort of rotation system amongst themselves, although they were clearly overestimating my daily intake. There were foil baking tins and Styrofoam take-out boxes and CorningWare casserole dishes (which unfortunately would need washing and returning), all lined up in a row and plastered with strips of adhesive tape letting me know whom to thank. *Thinking of you! The Ushers.* And *Bake uncovered at 350° till brown and bubbling, Mimi.* I would unlock the front door and bend to maneuver it all inside. From there I conveyed the items one by one to the kitchen, leaving my cane behind whenever I needed both hands for something spillable. I set everything next to the sink before I began adding to the list I kept on the counter. A column of previous offerings nearly filled the page: *Sue Borden—deviled eggs. Jan Miller—some kind of curry.* The earliest names were crossed out to show I'd already sent thank-you notes to them.

I must remember to buy more stamps. I was using a good many, these days.

After I'd recorded each dish, I dumped it in the garbage. I hated to waste food, but my refrigerator was packed to the gills and I didn't know what else to do. So the chicken salad, the ziti casserole, the tomatoes with pesto—dump, dump, dump. You could think of it as eliminating the middleman: straight from stoop to trash bin, without the intermediate pause on the kitchen table. Occasionally, abstractedly, I would intercept a drumstick or a sparerib and gnaw on it as I went about my work. While I rinsed out a Pyrex baking dish, I made my way through a cheesecake parked beside the sink, although I didn't much like cheesecake and this one was getting slimier every time I reached for a chunk with my wet fingers. And then, all at once, I was stuffed and my teeth had that furred feel from eating too much sugar, even though I hadn't sat down to an actual meal.

I dried the baking dish and set it out on the stoop with a Post-it attached: MIMI. Outside it was barely twilight, that transparent green kind of twilight you see at the end of a summer day, and I could hear children calling and a wisp of music from a passing car radio. I stepped back into the hall and closed the door.

Next, the mail, which shingled the hall floor and posed a

hazard to life and limb every time I stepped over it. I gathered it all up and took it back to the kitchen. The kitchen was my living room now. I'd done nothing about my plans to alter the guest room. I used the table as my desk, with my checkbook and my address book and various stationery supplies arranged in a row across one end. Oh, I was keeping up with my responsibilities admirably! I paid my bills the day they arrived, not waiting for the due-dates. I promptly filed catalogues and fliers in the recycling bin. I opened every sympathy note and read it with the utmost care, because there was always the chance that somebody would give me an unexpected glimpse of my wife. Somebody from her workplace, for instance: *Dr. Rosales was extremely qualified, and she will be missed at the Radiology Center.* Well, that was an added viewpoint that I very much appreciated. Or a former patient: *I was so sorry to read about ~~the death of your your loss~~ Dr. Rosales in the paper. She was very helpful to me after I had my ~~mastecto~~ surgery, answering all my questions and treating me ~~so normally so ordinarily~~ with dignity.* I suspected that this was a first draft mailed by mistake, but that just made it all the more meaningful, because it revealed the patient's sincerest feelings. She had valued the same qualities in Dorothy that I had valued: her matter-of-fact attitude, her avoidance of condescension. That was the Dorothy I'd fallen in love with.

I answered each note immediately.

Dear Dr. Adams,
Thank you so much for your letter. You were very kind to write.

Sincerely,
Aaron Woolcott

Dear Mrs. Andrews,
Thank you so much for your letter. You were very
kind to write.

Sincerely,
Aaron Woolcott

Then on to the food brigade:

Dear Mimi,
Thank you so much for the ziti casserole. It was
delicious.

Sincerely,
Aaron

Dear Ushers,
Thank you so much for the cheesecake. It was
delicious.

Sincerely,
Aaron

After that, the housework. Plenty to keep me busy there.

Sweeping the front hall, first. That was unending. Every morning when I woke up and every evening when I came home, a fresh layer of white dust and plaster chips covered the hall floor. At times there were also tufts of matted gray fuzz. What on earth? An outmoded type of insulation, I decided. I stopped sweeping and peered up into the rafters. It was a sight I looked quickly away from, like someone's innards.

And then the laundry, exactly twice a week—once for whites and once for colors. The first white load made me feel sort of lonely. It included two of Dorothy's shirts and her sensible cotton underpants and her seersucker pajamas. I had to wash and dry and fold them and place them in the proper drawers and align the corners and pat them down and smooth them flat. But the loads after that were easier. This wasn't an unfamiliar task, after all. It used to fall to whichever one of us felt the need of fresh clothing first, and that was most often me. Now I liked going down the stairs to the cool, dim basement, where there wasn't the least little sign of the oak tree. Sometimes I hung around for a while after I'd transferred the wet laundry from the washer to the dryer, resting my palms on the dryer's top and feeling it vibrate and grow warm.

Then a bit of picking up in the kitchen and the bedroom. Nothing major. Dorothy had been the clutterer in our family. By now I had retrieved several pieces of her clothing from around the room, and I'd returned her comb and her hay-fever pills to the medicine cabinet. I made no attempt to discard things. Not yet.

Over the course of an evening the phone would ring several times, but I always checked the caller ID before I picked up. If it was Nandina, I might as well answer. She would arrive at my door in person if I didn't let her know I was still among the living. But the Millers, always after me to go to the symphony with them, or the eternal Mimi King . . . Fortunately, I'd had the good sense to deactivate the answering machine. For a while I'd left it on, and the guilty burden of unreturned calls almost did me in before I remembered the *Off* button.

"I'm fine," I'd tell Nandina. "How are *you* since five o'clock, when I last saw you?"

"I can't imagine how you're coping there," she would say. "Where do you sit, even? How do you occupy your evening?"

"I have several places to sit, and no shortage of occupations. In fact, at this very minute I— Oh-oh! Gotta go!"

I would hang up and look at my watch. Only eight o'clock?

I angled my wrist to make sure the second hand was still moving. It was.

Occasionally, the doorbell would ring. Oh, how I hated that doorbell. It was a golden-voiced, two-note chime: *ding* dong. Kind of churchy, kind of self-important. But I felt compelled to answer it, because my car was parked out front and it was obvious I was home. I would sigh and make my way to the hall. Most often it was Mary-Clyde Rust. Not Jim, so much. Jim seemed to be having trouble these days thinking what to say to me, but Mary-Clyde was not in the least at a loss. "Now, Aaron," she would tell me, "I know you don't feel like company, so I won't intrude. But I need to see if you're all right. Are you all right?"

"I'm fine, thanks."

"Okay, good. Glad to hear it."

And she would nod smartly and spin on her heel and leave.

I preferred the neighbors who avoided me. The people who gazed suddenly elsewhere if they happened to be walking their dogs past when I stepped out of the house in the morning. The people who got into their cars with their backs kept squarely, tactfully turned in my direction as I got into my own car.

One evening when the doorbell rang it was a man I didn't know, a keg-shaped man with a short brown beard and a mop of gray-streaked brown hair. "Gil Bryan," he told me. "General contractor," and he handed me a business card. The outside light bulb made the sweaty skin beneath his eyes shine in a way I found trustworthy; that was the only reason I didn't just shut the door again. He said, "I'm the guy who put the tarp on your roof."

"Oh, yes."

"I see you haven't got it repaired yet."

"Not yet," I said.

"Well, that's my card, if you ever want someone to do it."

"Thanks."

"I know it must be the last thing on your mind right now."

"Well, thanks," I said, and then I did shut the door, but slowly, so as not to give offense. I liked the way he'd worded that. Even so, I just tossed his card into the porcelain bowl, because I was purposely ignoring the roof the way I had ignored those doctors peeking into the waiting room. "Roof? What roof?" I should have asked Mr. Bryan. "I don't see anything wrong with the roof."

The earliest bedtime I allowed myself was 9 p.m. I told myself I would read a while before I turned out the light; I wouldn't go to sleep immediately. I had a huge, thick biography of Harry Truman that I'd begun before the accident. But I couldn't seem to make much headway in it. "Reading is the first to go," my mother used to say, meaning that it was a luxury the brain dispensed with under duress. She claimed that after my father died she never again picked up anything more demanding than the morning paper. At the time I had thought that was sort of melodramatic of her, but now I found myself reading the same paragraph six times over, and still I couldn't have told you what it was about. My eyelids would grow heavier, and all at once I'd be jerking awake as the book slid off the bed and crashed to the floor.

So I would reach for the remote control and turn on the TV that sat on the bureau. I would watch—or stare in a glazed way at—documentaries and panel discussions and commercials. I would listen to announcers rattling off the side effects of all the medications they were touting. "Oh, sure," I would tell them. "I'll run out and buy that tomorrow. Why let a little uncontrollable diarrhea put me off, or kidney failure, or cardiac arrest?"

Dorothy used to hate it when I talked back like that. "Do you mind?" she would ask. "I can't hear a word they're saying."

This TV was just a little one, the little extra one that we sometimes watched the late news on when we were getting ready for bed. Our big TV was in the sunporch. It was an old Sony Trinitron. Jim Rust told me in the hospital that that was what had crushed Dorothy's chest; the firemen said it had fallen off its bracket high in the corner. Sony Trinitrons are known for their unusual weight.

A while back, Dorothy and I had discussed buying one of those new-fangled flat-screen sets, but we'd decided we couldn't afford it. If we had had a flat-screen TV, would Dorothy still be alive?

Or if her patient hadn't canceled. Then she wouldn't even have been home yet when the tree fell.

Or if she had stayed in the kitchen instead of heading for the sunporch.

If I'd said, "Let's see if *I* can find those Triscuits," and gone out to the kitchen to help her look, and then sat with her at the kitchen table while she ate them.

But no, no. I had to stomp off in a huff and sulk in the bedroom, as if it had mattered in the least that she'd refused to settle for Wheat Thins.

Oh, all those annoying habits of hers that I used to chafe at—the trail of crumpled tissues and empty coffee mugs she left in her wake, her disregard for the finer points of domestic order and comfort. Big deal!

Her tendency to make a little too much of her medical degree when she was meeting new people. "I'm Dr. Rosales," she would say, instead of "I'm Dorothy," so you could almost see the white coat even when she wasn't wearing one. (Not that she actually met new people all that often. She had never seen the purpose in socializing.)

And those orthopedic-type shoes she had favored: they had struck me, at times, as self-righteous. They had seemed a deliberate demonstration of her seriousness, her high-mindedness—a pointed reproach to the rest of us.

I liked to dwell on these shortcomings now. It wasn't only that I was wondering why they had ever annoyed me. I was hoping they would annoy me still, so that I could stop missing her.

But somehow, it didn't work that way.

I wished I could let her know that I'd kept vigil in the hospital. I hated to think she might have felt she was going through that alone.

And wouldn't she have been amused by all these casseroles!

That was one of the worst things about losing your wife, I found: your wife is the very person you want to discuss it all with.

The TV infiltrated my sleep, if you could call this ragged semi-consciousness sleep. I dreamed the war in Iraq was escalating, and Hillary Clinton was campaigning for the Democratic nomination. I rolled over on the remote control and someone all at once shouted, ". . . this stainless-steel, hollow-ground, chef-quality . . . ," by which time I was sitting bolt upright in my bed, my eyes popping and my heart pounding and my mouth as dry as gauze. I turned off the TV and lay flat again. I closed my eyes and gritted my teeth: *Go to sleep, damn it.*

You would think I'd have dreamed about Dorothy, but I didn't. The closest I came to it was the whiff of isopropyl alcohol that I hallucinated from time to time as I finally drifted off again. She had carried that scent home on her skin at the end of every workday. Early in our marriage I used to have vivid dreams about childhood doctor visits and vaccinations and the like, evoked by the alcohol scent as I lay sleeping next to her. Now the ghost of it brought me sharply awake, and once or twice I even spoke her name aloud: "Dorothy?"

But I never got an answer.

The casseroles started thinning out and the letters stopped. Could people move on that easily? Yes, well, of course. New tragedies happened daily. I had to acknowledge that.

It seemed heartless that I should think to go in for my semi-annual dental checkup, but I did. And then I bought myself some new socks. Socks, of all things! So trivial! But all my old ones had holes in the toes.

One evening my friend Nate called—WEISS N I on my caller ID. Him I picked up for. Right off I said, "Nate! How've you been?" without waiting for him to announce himself. But that was evidently a mistake, because I caught a brief hesitation before he said, "Hello, Aaron." Very low-voiced, very lugubrious; not at all his usual style.

"How about a game tomorrow?" I asked him.

"Pardon?"

"A game of racquetball! I'm turning into an old man here. All my joints are rusting."

"Well, ah, but . . . I was calling to invite you to dinner," he said.

"Dinner?"

"Yes, Sonya was saying we ought to have you over."

Sonya must be his wife. I had never met his wife. I suppose he must have mentioned her from time to time, but we didn't have that kind of friendship. We had a *racquetball* friendship. We'd gotten acquainted at the gym.

I said, "Over to . . . to your house, you mean?"

"Right."

"Well, gosh, Nate, I don't know. I don't even know where you live!"

"I live in Bolton Hill," he said.

"And also I just . . . It's been really busy at work lately. You wouldn't believe how busy. I barely have time for a sandwich, and then, when I do find time, there is so much extra food in the fridge, these—these—these casseroles and these . . . cheesecakes. It's practically a full-time job just to g-g-get it all d-d-d—just to eat it!"

"I see," he said.

"But thanks."

"That's okay."

"Tell Sonya I appreciate the thought."

"Okay."

I wanted to revisit the racquetball idea, but after I'd made such a point of being busy I figured that would be a mistake. So I just told him goodbye.

Not half an hour later, the phone rang again. This time it was TULL L. I answered, but I was warier now. All I said was, "Hello?"

"Hi, Aaron, it's Luke."

"Hi, Luke."

"I can understand why you might prefer not to go to Nate's."

"Excuse me?"

"He told me you'd turned down his invitation."

I said, "You're talking about Nate Weiss."

"Why, yes."

"You *know* Nate Weiss?"

"We met in the hospital waiting room, remember? When we both stopped by to visit."

This had been happening a lot lately. I swear I had no recollection that either one of them had stopped by, let alone that they'd met each other. But I said, "Oh. Right."

"He says he got the impression you're not up yet for coming to dinner."

"No, but racquetball . . ." I said. "I'm itching for a good game of racquetball."

There was a pause. Then Luke said, "Unfortunately, I don't know how to play racquetball."

"Oh."

"But I was thinking: if getting together with wives and such is too much to handle just now—"

"*Oh,* no. *Lord,* no," I said briskly. "Doesn't faze me in the least."

Another pause. Then he said, "I was thinking you could come to the restaurant instead."

He meant *his* restaurant, which was how we'd been introduced, back in the era of *The Beginner's Book of Dining Out*. I said, "Well, that's a good idea, Luke. Maybe sometime in the—"

"Just you and me and Nate; just us guys. No wives. We could have an early supper, and then you could head on home whatever time you felt like. How about it?"

I didn't want to do that, either, but what could I say? It was nice of him to make the effort. It was nice of both of them. I doubted I would have done as much if I had been in their place. I was more the "Let's move on" type. The "Maybe if I don't mention your loss, you'll forget it ever happened" type.

I kind of wished *they* were that type, to be honest.

But okay: might as well get this over with. I met them directly after work the next evening, a rainy, blowy Tuesday in mid-September. It had been pouring all day, and driving conditions were terrible. On top of that, I had trouble finding a parking space. By the time I walked into the restaurant (white linens, wide-planked floors, a certain worn-around-the-edges friendliness), Nate and Luke were already seated at a table. They made an unlikely pair. Nate looked very sleek and dark and professional in his black lawyer-suit, whereas Luke was one of those all-one-color, beige-hair-beige-skin types in shabby khakis, going a little soft around the middle. They seemed to be having no trouble finding things to talk about, though, if you judged by the way they'd set their heads together. I had the distinct impression that it was me they were talking about. How to deal with me, what topics would be safe to discuss with me. I'd barely pulled my chair out before Nate asked, "What about this *weather*, hey?" in a sprightly tone I wasn't familiar with. And Luke rode right over the tail of that with "You been following the Orioles?"

I felt compelled to answer in kind, in a louder voice than usual and with more verve. "You know, I *haven't* as a matter of fact been following the Orioles lately," I said, and then I wanted to take the words back, because I knew they'd be misinterpreted.

Sure enough: Nate said, "Well, of course you haven't. You've had a lot more important things to think about."

"No, I just meant—"

"Both of you should try the oysters!" Luke broke in. "We're in the *R* months now!"

Luke was such a quiet man ordinarily that it was bizarre to see him so animated. Besides which, he clearly felt uneasy sitting idle in his own workplace. He kept glancing around at other tables, raising his eyebrows significantly at waiters, frowning over Nate's head in the direction of the kitchen. "I personally recommend eating these raw," he told me in a distracted way, "but if you prefer, you could order the, uh . . . ," and then he paused to listen to what a short man in a stained apron was whispering in his ear.

". . . the Oysters Rockefeller," Nate finished for him. "Those are great. They use this special slab bacon that comes from upstate New York."

"You've eaten here before?" I asked.

"Yes, we came by last week," he said, and then he gave a little grimace, which I couldn't figure out for a moment. Was it because he had let it slip that he and Luke had met earlier, perhaps to cogitate over The Aaron Problem? No, on second thought it must have been the "we" that had embarrassed him, because next he said, as if correcting himself, "I had thought after I met him that I'd like to try his food."

So apparently the plan tonight was to avoid all mention of wives. Pretend neither one of them even possessed a wife. For now Luke, turning back to us as the aproned man left, said, "Sorry, the chef has run out of lamb chops, is all," and I happened to know that he was married to the chef. Under ordinary circumstances, he would have said that Jane or Joan or whatever her name was had run out of lamb chops, and he might also have brought her out to introduce her. But these were not ordinary circumstances.

I became perverse. I do that, sometimes. I started mentioning wives right and left—each utterance of the word "wife" thudding onto our table like a stone. "Did your wife like the Oysters Rockefeller, too?" I asked Nate, and Nate shifted in his seat and said, "Oh, um . . . she doesn't eat shellfish."

"You know, I've never thought to wonder," I said to Luke. "Did your wife become chef here before you married her, or after?"

"Er, before, actually," Luke told me. "Say! We need to decide on the wine!" And he sat forward urgently and beckoned to a waiter.

But I relented, after that, and let the conversation drift into more or less normal channels. Nate turned out to be the food-for-food's-sake type, going on at length about the breeding beds of oysters and the best source for heirloom pork. Luke, whom you'd expect to be deeply concerned with such things, didn't seem all that interested and spent most of his time focusing on what everyone else in the place was eating, or not eating enough of, or looking dissatisfied with. And within a bearable length of time, we managed to get through the evening.

"We should do this again!" Nate said as we were parting, and Luke said, "Yes! Make a regular thing of it!"

Oh, or else not. But I nodded enthusiastically, and shook both their hands, and thanked Luke for the meal, which he had refused to let us pay for.

I didn't thank either one of them for the event itself—for the act of getting together. That would have implied that it had been a charitable gesture of some sort, and I most certainly was not in need of charity.

So I turned up my collar, and gave both of them a jaunty wave of my cane, and set off through the downpour as cocky as you please.

Though I'd have to say that I felt a little, maybe, woebegone as I drove home alone.

The outside light was supposed to come on automatically at dusk, but the bulb must have burned out. A damned nuisance in the rain. I stepped in a couple of puddles as I was walking up the sidewalk to my house, and my trouser cuffs were already wet enough as it was. I unlocked the door and reached inside to turn the hall light on, but that was burned out, too. And when I pushed the door wider open, I met with some kind of resistance. A gravelly sound startled me. I peered down at the dark hall floor and made out several white and irregular objects. I nudged them with my foot. Rocks? No, plaster, chips of plaster. I pushed the door harder and it opened a few more inches. My eyes had adjusted by now. Against the black of the floor I saw scatterings of white and then a mound of white—pebbles and clods and sheets of white. And now that I thought about it, the air I was breathing was full of dust. I could feel an urge to cough pressing my throat. And I heard a loud, steady dripping from somewhere inside the house.

I closed the door again. I went back to my car, stepping in the same two puddles on the way, and got behind the steering wheel, where I spent several minutes collecting my thoughts. Then I drew a deep, shaky breath and fitted my key into the ignition.

And that is how it happened that I went to live with my sister.

4

Nandina lived in the house we'd grown up in, a brown-shingled foursquare north of Wyndhurst. Even in the rain, it was only a five-minute drive. I almost wished it were longer. When I got there I parked out front, but then I stayed in the car a minute, debating how I should word this. I didn't want to confess the true state of my house, because Nandina had been nagging me for weeks now to get started on the repairs. But if I just showed up with no explanation and asked for my old room back, she would think I was having a nervous breakdown or something. She would turn all motherly and there-there. She would be *thrilled*.

Well. As sometimes happens, she surprised me. She opened the front door when I rang and she sized up the situation—my slicked hair, damp clothes, the flecks of white plaster clinging to my trouser cuffs—and then she said, "Come in and stand on the mat while I fetch a towel."

"I've got—got a little water in my front hall," I told her.

She was heading toward the kitchen now, but she called back, "Take your shoes off and leave them there."

"I was thinking maybe, just for tonight—"

But she had disappeared. I stood dripping on the mat, breathing in the smells of my childhood—Johnson's paste wax and musty wallpaper. Even in the daytime the house was dark, with its small, oddly placed windows and heavy fabrics, and tonight it looked so dim that I kept feeling the need to blink to clear my vision.

"Your shoes, Aaron. Take off your shoes," Nandina said, returning. She had a faded dishtowel with her. She waited while I shucked my shoes off and removed my brace, and then she handed me the towel. It was one of those calendar towels our mother used to hang above the kitchen table. *1975,* it said. I mopped my face and then my hair. Nandina said, "Where's your cane?"

"I don't know."

"Did you leave it in the car?"

"Maybe."

"Did you bring any clothes with you?"

"No."

She stepped a bit closer, although she knew better than to offer an arm, and we made our way into the living room. She smelled of shampoo. She was wearing a gingham housecoat. (My sister was one of the last remaining women in America who changed into a housecoat at the end of every workday.) She waited for me to get settled on the couch, and then she said, "I'm going to see if you have any slippers here."

I probably did. I had plenty of other stuff. Our mother had never cleared my room out after I left home.

While Nandina was upstairs, I slumped back on the couch and gazed up at the ceiling. It was a really solid ceiling, the old-fashioned, cream plaster kind with a medallion in the center, not so much as a hairline crack anywhere in view.

I thought about the car my college roommate used to drive, a rusty heap of a Chevy that kept sputtering out for no reason. One day it died altogether, and he got out and unscrewed the license plate and walked away from it; never looked back. I wished I could do that with my house. I wouldn't miss a single thing about it. Let it vanish from the face of the earth. It wouldn't bother me in the least.

Nandina came back with a pair of corduroy moccasins that I'd completely forgotten. Then she brought me my brace, which I strapped on before I fitted my feet into the moccasins. "Now," Nandina said. "Have you had supper?"

"Oh, yes."

"Aaron," she said.

"What?"

"Tell the truth, now."

"I've had half a dozen raw oysters, a crab cake, garlic mashed potatoes, a Green Goddess salad, a seven-apple tart à la mode, and two glasses of wine."

"Goodness," Nandina said.

I tried not to look smug.

"And what, exactly," she asked, "is the current state of your house?"

"Ah." I considered. "Well, at the moment my hall ceiling seems to have taken on a bit of water."

"I see."

"It could happen to anyone," I told her. "It rained all last night, remember, and all today."

Nandina said, "It seems to me—"

"But we can t-t-talk about that to-tomorrow," I told her. "Meanwhile, I am *beat*. Are there sheets on my old bed?"

"Of course."

Yes, of course; why did I bother asking? I stood up and made a big show of yawning and stretching. "Guess I'll toddle off, then," I said. "Thanks for taking me in on such short notice. I promise I won't be in your hair more than a night or two."

"Aaron! You can stay here forever. You don't need to give me notice."

It shows how defeated I felt just then that the thought of staying forever seemed almost tempting.

My room was upstairs, at the rear of the house, next to Nandina's. (Which had been hers since childhood, although it would have made more sense if she'd taken over our parents' larger, brighter room after they died.) It was exactly as I'd left it when I went away to college. My model airplanes still lined the shelves; my vinyl recordings of U2 and Tom Petty were still stacked beneath the stereo. I found a pair of old pajama bottoms in the bureau, and I changed into them and then checked the bookcase for something to read myself to sleep with. But there I had less luck. All I saw were tattered collections of math games and logic puzzles. As a child I'd been good at those, although occasionally, when I ran into a wall (which was almost literally what it felt like—a kind of head-butting), I could become quite violent, throwing things and breaking things. When I cast my mind back to those scenes, I saw myself from outside: my spiky, flailing figure, my hair sticking out in all directions, while my mother stood at arm's length trying to calm me, trying to grab hold of me, murmuring ineffectual phrases. "Aaron, please. It's only a pastime. Take a little break and come back to it, why don't you?"

Where had all that passion gone? I wasn't like that now, thank heaven.

I used to be obsessed with magic tricks. I practiced them for days on end and then I'd start badgering the grownups. "Pick a card. Any card. Don't show me. Wait! You showed me what it was!"

And I wanted to make my living as a stand-up comic. I memorized jokes from magazines and then tried them out on relatives. "So, this man is walking down the street to the clock-repair shop, all bent over, with this great big grandfather clock on his back. He's taking it to be fixed, see. And he meets up with a friend, and the friend says—the friend says—"

But I never could get past that part without totally cracking up. I swear, I thought it was the most hysterical joke I had heard in all my life. "The friend says, 'Have you ever—have you ever—'"

I'd be breathless with laughter, weeping with laughter. My cheeks would be streaming with tears and my stomach would ache, and whichever aunts and uncles were listening would be smiling at me quizzically.

"'Have you ever thought of buying a *wristwatch*?'"

"A what?" they would ask, because by that point I was almost unintelligible. But even repeating it was a struggle, because I'd be rolling on the floor.

That I saw from outside now, too: my gleeful, sputtery self, with my arms wrapped around my rib cage and my whole body screwed up in an agony of hilarity.

It was no wonder I'd never had children. They would have made me too sad.

When Dorothy and I were courting, we barely talked about children. I believe Dorothy mentioned once or twice that she wasn't interested, but you couldn't call that a real discussion. So now there would be no next generation, because I didn't picture Nandina pairing off at this late date. The line would end with the two of us.

It was probably just as well, I figured.

"You didn't realize anything had changed," my mother told me. "You rode back from the hospital all happy and bouncy and glad to be going home, and you scrambled out of the backseat before either of us could reach for you—"

"I don't want to hear," I said.

"—and your leg just crumpled under you and you sat down hard on the sidewalk, but you didn't cry. You were trying to smile, but only one side of your mouth turned up, and you looked toward the two of us with this confused expression on your face but you were still trying to—"

I said, "Mom! Stop! I don't want to hear, I told you!"

She could be sort of obtuse, our mother. I know she wanted only the best for me, but still, it seemed to me I spent my childhood trying to fend her off. It was "No!" and "Go away!" and "I can do it myself!" I never headed out the door without her calling after me, "Don't forget your cane!"

"I don't need my cane."

"You *do* need your cane. Do you remember what happened last week at Memorial Stadium?"

I would set my teeth and draw to a halt, facing the street, until she arrived behind me with my cane.

She died in 1998, just six months after our father. Heart attacks, both of them. Now, when I looked back to all her fluttering and hovering, it didn't seem so bad. It seemed touching. But I knew that if she were to appear at that moment and ask what I could be thinking, getting into bed in the T-shirt I'd worn all day, I would snap at her once again: "Back off, I tell you! I'm fine!"

I fell asleep almost instantly, the first time I'd done that since Dorothy died. I dreamed that Jimmy Vantage still lived next door, although in fact he'd moved away at the end of seventh grade. We went to Stony Run to look for turtles. But Jimmy walked too fast for me, and I couldn't keep up. At one point I was actually crawling on the sidewalk and shouting for him to slow down. Which was odd, because in my dreams I tend to be assertively able-bodied. I practically have wings. But in this particular dream I was twisted into knots, hampered and gasping for air, and when I woke up I thought for an instant that I could still feel the grit from the sidewalk on my palms.

Nandina said she knew just whom to call: Top Hat Roofers. They'd been replacing the slates on our parents' house for as long as she could remember, she said, and she was sure they would understand that this should be given priority. "I'm going to phone them today," she told me. "And you, meanwhile, should call your insurance agent. Or have you already done that?"

"Um . . ."

She gave me an ultra-patient look, an "I know *you,* buster" look. I was not a fan of that look. We were seated at the kitchen table with tea and cornflakes—our family's traditional breakfast, which I had exchanged years ago for coffee and toast—and she had a memo pad in front of her that she was making notes on. I was not a fan of her memo pads, either. I said, "Forget it. I've got everything under control."

"What do you mean by 'everything'?"

"I mean the insurance agent, the roof . . . and it's going to be way more than just the roof. Shows how much *you* know about it. I need a general contractor."

"And you have one?" she asked.

"Of course."

She looked unconvinced.

I said, "His name is . . ." Then I started over again, like someone retracing his steps to take a long, running jump. "His name is . . . Gil Bryan."

It was the image of the shining skin beneath his eyes that brought it forth, finally. I said, "I'll just give him a call today to let him know about the hall ceiling."

"Well," Nandina said. "All right, I guess."

She seemed almost disappointed.

We drove downtown in separate cars, at my insistence. I said, "Who knows? We might want to leave at different times."

"I don't mind adjusting my schedule."

"But also," I said, "I may run by the house after work for a few of my things."

"You want me to come with you?"

"No."

In fact, I had no intention of going to my house. I had cased the bureau and the closet in my old room and found more than enough clothes to suit my purposes, provided I wasn't too picky: stretched-out, kiddie-looking underpants, and jeans that fit fine although they seemed a bit high in the waist, and a button-down oxford shirt that I remembered from eighth grade. You would think oxford shirts would be timeless, but this one was kind of spindly in the collar. Well, never mind. For shaving, I'd made do with a disposable plastic razor I found among Nandina's backup supplies in the bathroom. I use an electric shaver, as a rule. I made a mental note to buy a new one on my lunch break.

That was the first time I admitted to myself that I couldn't face the sight of my house: when I realized I was willing to spring for a new electric shaver rather than retrieve my old one from my medicine cabinet.

So, as soon as I reached work, I shut myself in my office and started making phone calls. First I left a message on the answering machine at my insurance company—just the company in general, because I had no recollection as to who my personal agent was, never having had to use him. Then I searched the Internet for *gil bryan contractor baltimore*. No Gil to be found, but there was a Bryan Bros. General Contracting Co. I tried that number, and this time I reached an actual human being. "*Hell*-o," a man said, too loudly.

"Bryan Brothers?"

"Yep."

"Gil Bryan?"

"Nope."

"But you *have* a Gil Bryan."

"Yep."

"Could I speak to him, please?"

"He's out."

"Could I leave him a message?"

"Let me give you his cell."

I wrote the number down, but I didn't try it right away. The conversation with the first guy had worn me out.

How about if I just sold my house? Put it on the market as a "fixer-upper." (I'll say!) Paid somebody to pack my belongings so I wouldn't have to set foot in the place ever again. Surely there were people you could hire to do that. I would rent a little apartment, fully furnished. If anything happened to that one, I'd rent another.

The birdwatching book had gone off to Irene, and I was working on one of our vanity titles: George S. Hogan, Sr.'s *My War.* In the office, we referred to it as *War Thirteen.* Why was it that so many men viewed their military service as the defining event of their lives? They could have lived ninety years or more, they could have had several marriages and half a dozen children and outstandingly successful careers, but still, if they chose one experience to sum them up, it would be Vietnam, or Korea, or the Normandy invasion. It was especially hard to fathom in the case of Mr. Hogan, because his own particular war sounded downright dull. *My best buddy in the barracks was Cy Helm. He was a really fine fellow. You couldn't ask for a finer fellow than old Helm I always tell folks.*

Apart from inserting a comma after *old Helm,* I left the text alone. That was our policy with the vanity manuscripts. (Some people didn't even want the commas added.) I waded through another three pages, and then I rubbed my eyes and stretched and got up to fetch a cup of coffee.

Charles was playing FreeCell on his computer. He was a stocky, rumpled man with a perennially red face, slightly older than the rest of us, and he had his own mysterious schedule that none of us interfered with. Irene seemed to be out of the office, and Peggy was refilling the cream pitcher. "Oh, poor Aaron," she said when she saw me. "I heard about your ceiling."

I sent a malevolent glare toward Nandina's office door.

"Who are you hiring to fix it?" she asked.

"Just this guy."

"Because I know a good—"

"Never mind; it's all seen to," I said.

Then I added, "Thanks anyhow," because I might have sounded a little abrupt.

Peggy didn't seem to take offense. She passed me the cream pitcher, handle first, and asked, "How's Mr. Hogan's book coming along?"

"He's got this really fine buddy I'm reading about," I told her. "*Really* fine. You know: just a really, really fine buddy."

Peggy smiled at me. She was one of those people without any sense of irony. (Well, unless you counted her Little Miss Muffet clothing style, which I sometimes suspected you *could* count.) Still, it seemed I had to go on now that I was wound up. "It could be worse, I suppose," I said. "It could be *My Years with the City Council*. That's my gold standard."

Then Charles weighed in, from his desk across the room. "I'd vote for *The Life of an Estate Lawyer*, myself," he called, without taking his gaze from the computer screen.

"Oh, good point. How could I have overlooked *that* one?"

"Remember *The Beginner's Book of Kitchen Remodeling*?" Peggy asked me.

"Ye-e-es," I said. It hadn't stuck in my mind, especially.

"I was thinking you might find that helpful when you're dealing with your house repairs."

"Whoa!" I said. "Actually *consult* one of our books?"

She nodded, solemnly.

"Good heavens," I said. "Those books are not meant to be used."

"They're not?"

"Well, not in any serious way. They're more like . . . gestures. Things you give to other people."

"But in *Kitchen Remodeling* they talk about what you should settle with the contractor first, before he starts work. I was thinking that would be good to know."

The "they" she referred to was me, as it happened—me and a retired kitchen designer from Anne Arundel County. So I just said, "Oh. True," and took my coffee back to my office without the slightest thought of following her suggestion.

"Remind him it's a buyer's market before you settle on the price," Charles called after me. "Buyer's? Seller's? Whichever."

"Okay."

Mr. Hogan was describing field maneuvers. *Smith and Donaldson were positioned on my left about fifty yards away and Merritt and Helm were holed up in the woods to my right but I didn't have a visual on them because there was a considerable dip in the terrain running some two hundred yards north-northeast along the . . .*

My eyes wandered toward my bookcase. The *Beginner's* series lined several shelves—a rainbow of narrow, shiny spines identical in size. I stood up and went to examine them more closely. They were arranged by publication date, earliest to the most recent. *Kitchen Remodeling* dated from several years back, and it was on the top shelf. I pulled it out.

"Knowing What You Want" was the first chapter. *(Where in your present kitchen do you do your slicing and dicing? DO you, in fact, do any slicing and dicing?)* "Communicating with Your Contractor" was the second. Almost the entire remainder of the book consisted of what now seemed to me an inordinately detailed plan for setting up an interim kitchen in a spare bathroom.

I took the book to my desk and sat down to read the contractor chapter. Apparently the essential element was control. *Do not assume that, having issued your directives, you can lean back and let your contractor run wild. Inform him or her that you will be checking his or her progress at the end of every workday. Insist that he or she submit a timeline, in writing, outlining the steps to be completed by certain fixed dates. Schedule meetings on a weekly basis, at which you will require him or her to present a record of current expenses.*

It was Nandina who was to blame for the him-her business, although otherwise she steered clear of the editing side of things. (For starters, she couldn't spell. She was one of the smartest women I knew, but she couldn't spell worth a damn.)

I closed the book on an index finger and reached for the telephone. I punched in the number I'd written down for Gil Bryan.

"Hello," he said.

At least he wasn't as gruff as the first man. He spoke at a normal level, above the whirr of some power tool in the background.

I said, "Gil Bryan?"

"Yes."

"This is Aaron Woolcott. I own that house on Rumor Road where the—where the—"

Stupidly, I could not seem to get the words out.

"Where the tree fell," Gil Bryan said. "Right."

But even with his help, I wasn't able to go on. I can't explain what happened. My eyes filled with tears and I didn't trust my voice.

"Are you thinking of getting that fixed?" he asked me after a moment.

I swallowed and said, "Yes."

"I could come by and take a look, if you like."

"I'm not there," I said. I cleared my throat.

"Maybe after you get home from work, then?"

"I mean, I'm not *ever* there. I'm staying with my sister. That rain we've had broke through the tarp and the hall ceiling fell in."

Gil Bryan made a whistling sound through his teeth.

"I was thinking," I said, "could you stop by my sister's house around five-thirty and I'd just give you the key so you could go check the place out?"

"Check it out on my own, you're saying?"

"Yes."

There was a pause. Then he said, "Well, I could do that, I guess. But it'd be better to have you along."

I said nothing.

"So, okay," he said. "I'll go it alone."

"Thanks."

"You're talking about just the roof? Or the interior, too."

"Everything. I don't know. Just take care of it. You decide."

"Everything? What kind of time frame are you looking for?"

"I have no idea," I said. "However much time it takes, I guess."

Then I gave him Nandina's address, and hung up, and put *The Beginner's Book of Kitchen Remodeling* back in its place on the shelf.

· · ·

I'd chosen five-thirty for a reason: Nandina would still be at work. She made it a point of honor, most evenings, to stay longer than anyone else in the office. So she wouldn't be there to horn in on my first consultation with Gil Bryan. She wouldn't find out that it *was* my first consultation.

But my sister has an uncanny sixth sense; I can't think of any other way to explain it. She knocked on my door at a quarter till five and stuck her head in and said, "I'm going now. See you at home."

"You're going *now*?"

"I might as well. I'm at a good stopping place," she said. She had her purse slung over her shoulder.

So, by the time I got there, she was already in the kitchen starting dinner preparations. And when the doorbell rang, she arrived in the hall right behind me, wiping her hands on the hem of the apron that covered her housecoat.

Gil Bryan had the dingy, dusty look of a man who'd been at hard labor all day, but the skin beneath his eyes was still shining, and I felt the same sense of trust that I had before. I said, "Come in, Mr. Bryan," and he said, "Gil."

"Aaron," I told him, and we shook hands. (He had a hand like a baseball mitt.) Then I had to add, "This is my sister, Nandina," because she was still standing there. "Contractor," I told her curtly, and she said, "Oh," and backed off and returned to the kitchen.

"Come in and have a seat," I said to Gil.

"Oh, I'm all dirty. I'll just take the key and be on my way."

I fished my key case out of my pocket. As I was unhooking my house key, I asked, "Are you planning on going over there this evening?"

"I figured I would."

"Because I'm not sure the electricity is working."

"Huh," he said. "Okay, I'll go in the morning. Check it out during daylight. How about I come by here tomorrow, same time, once I know what's what."

"Sounds good," I said. I handed him the key.

"And you want me looking at everything."

"Everything," I said. "Make a list."

"Okay, then," he said. But I could tell he was baffled by my attitude.

We shook hands again, and he left. Not two seconds later, Nandina popped out of the kitchen. "*That* didn't take long," she said.

"He just needed a key, was all."

She nodded, apparently satisfied, and returned to her cooking.

But over dinner she asked, "How exactly did you get this contractor's name?"

"Through Jim Rust," I told her.

She cocked her head, like someone who thought she'd heard an off-note in a song. She said, "Jim Rust has used his services personally?"

"Yes, of course," I said, although I didn't know that for a fact. Then I said, "It's a done deal, Nandina. Butt out."

"Well! *Sorry,*" she said.

We ate the rest of the meal without talking.

. . .

The following evening, I had Gil to myself. I was waiting at the house for him when he rang the doorbell.

"Hey there," he said, and I said, "Come on in."

This time, he had clean clothes on—a chambray shirt and fresh khakis—and he accepted the seat I offered him on the couch. I sat at the other end of it. He was holding a crisp white file folder, I was happy to see. It implied some degree of professionalism. He opened the folder on the coffee table and spread out an array of papers covered in surprisingly small, tidy, uppercase handwriting.

"So, okay, Aaron, here's what we've got," he said.

I was happy, too, that he used my first name. Workmen who persist in saying "Mr.," even after you've told them not to, always strike me as deliberately off-putting.

"You were right about the electric," he told me. "There's been a short in the wires, on account of the water dripping down through the walls to the basement. For that I'm going to bring in Watkins Wattage, but they can't make it over to take a look till—"

I heard the front door open. Nandina called, "Aaron?"

Damn. She appeared in the living-room entrance.

"Oh!" she said.

Gil stood up. "Evening," he said.

"Good evening."

"We're busy going over some figures," I told her.

I gave her a look that she couldn't possibly mistake, and she said, "Oh, all right; don't let me interrupt," and backed hastily out of the room.

"You were saying—?" I asked Gil.

He had sat down again, and he was riffling through his papers. "There's structural damage in the attic," he said. "That's the worst of it. Some of the rafters need replacing. Roof, of course, and the insulation's shot; and so are the hallway and kitchen ceilings and the cabinets on the west wall. Chimney will want rebuilding, too. Chimneys are kind of a big deal, I hate to say. Now, moving on to the sunporch—"

"Can't we just take that off?" I asked.

"Say what?"

"Take the sunporch off; demolish it. It's a lost cause, anyhow, and it was only tacked on to begin with. It's not a part of the main—"

"Would you two like some refreshment?" Nandina asked. She had reappeared, but from the dining room this time.

"No," I told her.

"Mr. Bryan?"

"Gil," he said. He had risen once more to his feet. "No, thanks."

"A cold beer, maybe?"

"No, thanks."

"Or a glass of wine?"

"Thanks anyway."

"We don't have anything harder," Nandina said. She had ventured a few feet farther into the room; any minute now she would plop herself down in an armchair, as if this were a topic that required deep discussion. "I know it's still gin-and-tonic weather, but—"

I said, *"Nandina."*

"What?"

"That's okay," Gil told her. "I don't drink."

"Oh."

"AA," he said. He straightened his back as he spoke, almost defiantly, but then he raised a hand to feel for his beard in this uncertain sort of manner.

Nandina said, "Oh, I'm sorry!"

"That's okay."

I was fully expecting Nandina to segue into the non-alcoholic side of the menu, but before she could, Gil told her, "We were just talking about the sunporch. Aaron here is saying how he wants to take it off."

"Take it off? Take it off of the house?"

"That's what he's been saying."

"Well, that makes no sense whatsoever," Nandina told me. "You'll lower the resale value."

I said, "What do I care about the resale value?"

"It's a tiny house as it is. You need that room."

"Nandina, do you mind? We're trying to have a private conversation."

"You're just *mad* at the sunporch; that's what it is."

"Mad!"

"You're just . . . emotional about it, because of what happened there."

"For God's sake, Nandina, what business is that of yours?"

"Here's a thought," Gil broke in. He spoke in an extra-quiet, reasonable-sounding voice, as if negotiating a treaty. "What if we were to keep the sunporch but change the orientation."

I said, "Orientation?"

"Like, right now it looks like you had a desk kind of arrangement along that wall of shelving that joins the house, am I right?"

The wall where the TV had hung, the one that killed her. I nodded.

He said, "How about we plan now for your desk to face the front, in the middle of the room. Better anyway, right? You'd be looking out on the front yard. And then we'd run a row of shelves all around the circumference, underneath the windows. Just low shelves, built in. It would be, like, a whole new different setup."

I said, "Well. I don't know."

Although I did see his point.

Which Nandina must have guessed, because she said, "Thank you, Mr. Bryan."

Then she turned and left us alone, finally, and Gil sat back down on the couch and we went on with his papers.

Mr. Hogan said he'd had an inspiration about his war book. He thought it should include his letters home to his mother. That was fine with me. We were merely his printers. But what I hadn't realized was that he meant to submit the letters in their original, handwritten form. He set them on my desk one day in early October: a three-inch stack of envelopes bound with a satin ribbon that had probably once been blue. "Now, here is an example," he said, slipping one envelope free. He hadn't even sat down yet, although I'd offered him a chair. He was a tiny, stooped, white-haired man with squarish patches of pink in his cheeks that made him look enthusiastic. He drew the letter from the envelope with his crabbed fingers. Even from where I stood, I could see that it was almost illegible: a penciled scrawl, faded to silver, on bumpy onionskin paper.

I said, "You'd have to get them typed, of course."

"Here I'm telling her all about what they give us to eat. I'm telling how I miss her fried shad and her shad roe."

"Mr. Hogan? Are you planning to have these typed?"

"I'm saying how I haven't had real biscuits since I left home."

"Who typed your original manuscript?" I asked him. It had arrived looking quite presentable, which wasn't something we could take for granted in our business. (And we didn't have even a hope of any sort of electronic submission.)

"That was my daughter-in-law did those," he told me.

"Could your daughter-in-law type these letters, too?"

"I don't want to ask her."

No point inquiring why, I supposed. People's goodwill wears out. It happens. I walked over to open my office door. "Peggy?" I called. "Could you bring in that list of professional typists?"

"Right away."

"Is this something I would have to pay for?" Mr. Hogan asked me.

"Well, yes."

"Because I'm not made of money, you know."

"I doubt it would be that expensive."

"I've already spent my life savings on this."

Peggy walked in, holding a sheet of paper. She seemed to be wearing a crinoline underneath her skirt. I didn't know you could even buy crinolines anymore. She asked, "How's the arthritis today, Mr. Hogan?"

"He says I'm going to have to get these letters typed," Mr. Hogan told her.

"Oh, well," Peggy said, "I've got a nice long list here of people who can help you with that."

"I don't think I can afford it."

Peggy glanced down at her list, as if she might find some solution there.

"These are letters I wrote to my mother," Mr. Hogan said, offering forth the one letter in both hands. "I thought they might add a little something to my story."

"Oh, letters from the front are *always* good," Peggy told him.

"Mine are more like, from Florida."

"Still," Peggy said.

"I write about how I miss her cooking. Her shad and her shad roe."

"I love shad roe," Peggy said.

I said, "Well, in any event—"

"I'm living on a fixed income," Mr. Hogan said. He was peering intently into Peggy's eyes, and the letter he held was trembling.

Peggy said, "I'll tell you what, Mr. Hogan. Why don't *I* just type them."

As if I hadn't seen that one coming.

"Would you charge me?" Mr. Hogan asked.

"Oh, no," she said. "It won't be any trouble."

"Well, thank you," he told her. A little too easily, in my opinion.

I said, "That's very nice of you, Peggy," but in a severe tone, as if I were reproving her.

It was wasted on both of them, though. Peggy merely dimpled at me, and Mr. Hogan was busy fitting his letter back in its envelope.

I always worried our older clients might feel insulted by Peggy. Her honeyed voice and her overly respectful manner could have been viewed as, let's say, patronizing. Condescending. *I* would have found her condescending. But no one else seemed to. Mr. Hogan placed his stack of letters in her hand quite happily, and then he said to me, with a combative lift of his chin, "I was sure it would all work out!"

Somehow, I had turned into the heavy. It wasn't the first time.

When Mr. Hogan had gone, I told Peggy, "I certainly hope you know what you've gotten yourself into."

"Oh, yes," she said blandly.

Then she offered to fetch me a cup of coffee, even though it was mid-afternoon. I never drank coffee in the afternoon, as she very well knew. She was just changing the subject.

If it hadn't been for Peggy, Dorothy would have found her Triscuits exactly where she had left them. I thought about that, sometimes. I turned it over in my mind: could I say that, if not for Peggy, Dorothy would still be alive? But it didn't really compute. Often, Dorothy had taken her six Triscuits to the sunporch with her. Most likely it would not have changed a thing if she had found them.

So I couldn't really hold that against Peggy. Although I seemed to hold *something* against her, these days. She was just so, what was it, so sweetie-sweet. And Irene was doing her best to avoid me, as if grief might be contagious, and Charles couldn't even meet my eyes. Oh, I was sick to death of my officemates.

Maybe I should take a vacation. But how would I fill my time, then? I didn't even have any hobbies.

"I should start volunteering or something," I told Peggy. "Sign on with some sort of charity. Except that I can't think of anything specific I could do."

Peggy seemed about to say something, but then she must have changed her mind.

My insurance agent's name turned out to be Concepción. How could I have forgotten *that*? She had more dealings with Gil than with me. I gave her Gil's cell-phone number and the two of them grew thick as thieves, conferring by e-mail and in person and faxing documents back and forth. Gil's file folder metamorphosed into a three-inch-thick, color-tabbed notebook stuffed with estimates, receipts, diagrams, and lists. He brought it over most evenings after supper and sat on the couch to lay papers the length of the coffee table, explaining his progress in a degree of detail that would have more than satisfied *The Beginner's Book of Kitchen Remodeling*. Already the damaged rafters had been replaced and the roof was nearly finished. He was aiming to beat the weather, he said. He would tackle the interior later, after it grew too cold to work outside. He had hired two extra carpenters and so far things were on schedule, as I would see for myself if I ever came to check it all out.

I said, "Maybe one of these days."

He looked at me for a moment. I thought he was going to start pressing me the way other people did (my sister, to be exact), but all he said, finally, was, "Okay."

"I mean, of course I'll stop in at some point."

"Sure," he said. "Meantime, I'll just keep on coming by here. It's no trouble."

Whom did he remind me of then? Oh, of course: Peggy. Peggy with Mr. Hogan, so let-me-help-you and tactful. He and Peggy would make a good couple, in fact. I had to grin at the picture of it: Peggy in her china-shepherdess crinoline, hand in hand with grizzly-bear Gil.

"Hey," I said. "Gil. Do you have a wife?"

He said, "Aw, no," in the bashful, head-ducking manner of someone deflecting a compliment.

"You've never been married?"

"Nope." He rubbed his beard. "I had a kind of misspent youth," he allowed after a moment. "Dropped out of college, got in with the wrong crowd . . . I guess I missed the window for getting married."

"Well, you certainly seem to have straightened yourself out."

"Believe me," he said, "if it wasn't for my cousin, I'd still be falling off of some barstool. My cousin Abner; he took me into his business. Saved my life, really."

"How about your brother?" I asked.

"What brother?"

"Isn't it Bryan Brothers General Contracting?"

"Well, yeah. But that's only because 'Bryan Cousins' wouldn't work."

"It wouldn't?"

"Think about it. Everybody'd call up on the phone: 'Could I speak to Mr. Cousins, please?'"

I laughed.

"No, I don't have any brothers," he said. "Just a bunch of sisters, always on my tail."

"*Tell* me about it," I said. "Sisters."

"Say," he said, as if seizing his chance. "Pardon me for mentioning this, but I've been wondering if you'd want to do something about your things."

"My things," I said.

"Your papers and such and your personal things that you left behind in your house. Your mail, even. Any time I walk in, there's mail all over your front-hall floor. It's no bother to *me,* bringing it over, but did you know you could just get online and notify the Post Office to start delivering here?"

"You're right," I said. "I'll do that."

"And then your kitchen items. Your dishes in the cupboards. Once we start to work inside, you'll want to box all that up and move it to the bedroom or someplace."

"I'll see to it," I told him.

"Your sister took the stuff from the fridge already, but there's other things, cereals and canned goods and things."

"My sister's been there?"

"Just to get the stuff from the fridge."

"I didn't know that," I said.

"I guess she didn't want to bother you with it."

I looked down at the sheet of expenses I was holding. I said, "I realize I must seem sort of unreasonable about going back to the house. It's just that I think I'd feel, maybe, overwhelmed or something."

He said, "Well. I get that."

"To tell the truth, I don't know if I'll *ever* want to go there."

"Oh, wait till you see how we fix it up," he told me. "I was thinking we might put a lighter shade of floorboard in the front hall. I mean, assuming you approved it."

"But even so," I said. "Even with lighter floorboards."

He waited, patiently, with his eyes fixed on mine.

"Hey!" I said. "You wouldn't want to buy the place, would

you? Buy it for, like, an investment? Once you get it fixed up you could make a tidy profit, I bet."

Then I gave a sort of laugh, in case he laughed himself. But he didn't. He said, "I don't have the money."

"Oh."

"Look," he said. "Don't worry about your stuff. I'll just have my guys box it up, as long as you don't mind them messing with it."

"Of course I don't mind," I told him. "I probably wouldn't miss it if they took it all to the dump."

"Oh, they won't do that. Then, anything we find that we think you might need here, I'll just bring it over in the truck the next time I come."

"Well, thanks," I said.

I cleared my throat.

I said, "One other thing . . ."

He waited.

I said, "Do you think you could bring me some clothes?"

"Clothes."

"Just whatever's in my closet, and the bureau across from my bed?"

"Huh," he said.

I gestured toward what I was wearing. So far I had been making do with the clothes I'd found in my old room, but there was no denying that I was dressed a bit too youthfully. "You could just throw it all in your truck bed," I said. "I'm not asking you to pack it up or anything."

"Well," he said, "we can handle that."

"Thank you," I said.

.   .   .

I knew I should have felt grateful to Nandina for making that fridge trip. (Even though I had no doubt there'd been an investigative element to it.) Oh, whenever I took the trouble to notice, I could see that I was surrounded by people who were doing their best to look out for me. It wasn't only Nandina. Charles brought me foil-wrapped loaves of his wife's banana bread, heavy as bricks. Irene left fliers on my desk for life-threatening adventures designed to take my mind off myself—hang-gliding and rock-climbing and coral-reef-diving. My ex-neighbors called frequently with dinner invitations, and when I made excuses they said, "O-ka-ay . . . ," in this reluctant drawl that implied they were letting me off the hook this time, but not forever. And Luke had turned our supper at the restaurant into an almost-weekly event, while Nate had reinstated our racquetball games at the gym.

But I wasn't all that good at gracious acceptance. Oh, especially not with Nandina. With Nandina I was constantly on the defensive, bristling at every intrusion and batting away her most well-meant remarks. Not that she didn't deserve some of this. The things she came up with! Once, for instance, she said, "At least you're not going to have to make any big domestic adjustments. I mean, seeing as how Dorothy never cooked your meals for you or anything."

("No," was my rejoinder to that, "we had a very equitable marriage. We treated each other like two competent adults.")

Or another time, when I undertook to do the laundry for the two of us: "No doubt *Dorothy* found it sufficient to split the wash into just whites and colors," she told me in a forbearing tone, "but as a rule we divide the colors, then, into pales and darks."

I didn't let on that Dorothy would more likely have thrown all three categories into one washer load and let it go at that.

More and more often I could hear my sister thinking, *It's too bad his wife had to die, but was she really worth quite this much grief? Does he have to go on and on about it?*

"You assume people won't notice if you skip a day's shaving or wear the same clothes all week," she said, "but they do. Betsy Hardy told me she crossed the street the other day when she saw you coming, because she thought you wouldn't want to be caught looking the way you did. I said, 'Well, you were sweet to be so considerate, Betsy, but frankly, I don't believe he'd even care.'"

"Betsy Hardy? I didn't see her."

"She saw *you,* is my point," Nandina said. "I thought you were planning to fetch some better-looking clothes from your house."

"Oh, Gil's going to bring those over."

"What: you mean you'd let him go through your belongings?"

"Well, yes."

She gave me a narrow-eyed look. "When Jim Rust recommended Gil," she said, "did he give you any clue to his background? Did he tell you what his history is? Where he's from? Is he a Baltimore person?"

"He's *fine,* Nandina. Take my word for it."

"I was just curious, is all."

"He never should have let you know that he was in AA."

"I don't have anything against AA."

"It's better than *not* being in AA if he ought to be," I pointed out.

"Well, of course it is. You think AA is why I asked about his background? I'm completely sympathetic to his being in AA! Why, every time he comes over I offer him fruit juice or lemonade."

"True," I said.

But I knew that was only because she'd caught him once with a can of Coke. Nandina had a real thing about soft drinks. She didn't just dislike them; she viewed them with moral outrage. If there were a twelve-step program for cola drinkers, I bet she would have sent them a hefty contribution.

Well, but listen to me. I had no business complaining about her. She had taken me in without hesitation when I didn't have anywhere else to go, and she hadn't shown the least annoyance at my upsetting her private routine. She was my closest living relative. We shared childhood memories that no one else had been part of.

Often, when we were by ourselves, one of us would start a sentence the way our father used to. "Needles to say . . ." we would begin—Dad's habitual little joke, if you could call it that. And the other one would smile.

Or when I was sorting through the porcelain bowl after Gil brought it over—the bowl from my front hall, with its layers of junk mail and take-out menus and random chits of paper. I spread it all on the kitchen table one night while Nandina was fixing supper, and there was Bryan Brothers' business card. I said, "Gilead!"

"What?"

"That's Gil's name: Gilead Bryan. I'd been assuming it was Gilbert."

Nandina stopped stirring the soup and said, "Gilead. Like the song?"

"Like the song," I said, and it was another "Needles to say" moment, because how many other people would come up with "There Is a Balm in Gilead"? It was our mother's favorite hymn, the one she sang when she washed the dishes, only I always thought it was a *bomb* in Gilead, and when one of our cousins made fun of me for singing it that way, Nandina cracked him over the head with a Monopoly board.

Living in this house again was not half bad, really. In a way it was kind of cozy.

At Christmastime, the company always made a big production out of one of our past titles, *The Beginner's Book of Gifts.* We arranged to have it displayed next to cash registers all over town, with a red satin bow tied around each copy. I myself felt the bow was illogical. After all, the book was *about* gifts; it was not a gift in itself. But Irene was very fond of the bow, which she had dreamed up several years back, and Charles claimed it went over well. Generally we deferred to Charles in matters of public taste. He was the only one of us who led what I thought of as a normal life—married to the same woman since forever, with triplet teenage daughters. He liked to tell little domestic-comedy, *Brady Bunch*-style anecdotes about the daughters, and the rest of us would hang around listening like a bunch of anthropologists studying foreign customs.

Nandina and I let Christmas pass almost unobserved. We had stopped exchanging gifts years ago, and apart from the balsam wreath that Nandina brought home from the supermarket we made no attempt to decorate. On Christmas Day we went to Aunt Selma's for dinner, as we had done since our childhood. Even my marriage hadn't changed that, although Dorothy and I had sworn every year that we would do something different the next time Christmas came around. The food was dismal, and the guest list had shrunk as various relatives died or moved away. This year there were just five at the table: Aunt Selma herself, Nandina and I, and Aunt Selma's son Roger with his much younger third wife, Ann-Marie. We had not seen Roger and Ann-Marie since the previous Christmas, so there was the issue of Dorothy's death to be waded through. Roger was one of those people in favor of pretending it hadn't happened. He was clearly embarrassed that I had had the bad taste to show up, even. But Ann-Marie plunged right in. "I was so, so sorry," she said, "to hear about Dorothy's passing."

"Thank you," I said.

"And *last* Christmas, she was looking so well!"

"Yes . . . she *was* well."

"How are you doing, though?" she asked me.

"I'm okay."

"I mean, really how."

"I'm doing all right, all things considered."

"I ask because my girlfriend?—Louise?—she just lost her husband."

"Oh, I'm sorry to hear that."

"He passed away yesterday morning. Leukemia."

"Yesterday!" Aunt Selma said. "Christmas Eve day?"

"Yes, and you just know she'll never celebrate a Christmas again that she won't be reminded of Barry."

"Also, it must make scheduling the funeral so awkward," Aunt Selma said.

"But, Aaron?" Ann-Marie asked. "Do you have any words of wisdom I might pass on to her?"

"Words of wisdom," I said.

"Like, how to handle the grieving process?"

"I wish I did," I said. "Afraid I can't be much help."

"Oh, well. I'll just tell her you seem to have survived it," she said.

Roger said, "Honestly, Ann-Marie!" as if surviving a loved one's death were somehow reprehensible. But the odd thing was, right at that moment I realized that I *had* survived it. I pictured Ann-Marie's friend waking up this morning, the first full day of her life without her husband, and I thanked heaven that I was past that stage myself. Even though I still felt a constant ache, I seemed unknowingly to have traveled a little distance away from that first unbearable pain.

I sat up straighter and drew a deep breath, and it was then that I began to believe that I really might make my way through this.

And yet, just two nights later, I had one of those dreamlike thoughts that drift past as you're falling asleep. *Why!* I thought. *Dorothy hasn't phoned me lately!*

She used to phone from her office during the early days of our marriage, just to say hello and see how my work was going. So the honeymoon was over, it seemed. I felt a little tug of regret, even though I knew it was only to be expected.

But then I came fully awake and I thought, *Oh. She's dead.*

And it wasn't any easier than it had been at the very beginning. *I can't do this,* I thought. *I don't know how. They don't offer any courses in this; I haven't had any practice.*

Really, I had made no progress whatsoever.

True winter arrived in mid-January. There was a snowfall of several inches, and then some weeks of bitter cold. But by that time the exterior work on my house was mostly finished and Gil's men had moved indoors. He told me they were replastering the ceilings now. "Oh, good," I said. I didn't go see for myself. Nandina did, though. She reported it to me afterward; said she had felt that somebody ought to make up for my rudeness. I said, "Rudeness? Who was I rude to?"

"The plasterers, of course," she said. "Workmen need to know that their work is appreciated. They did an excellent job on those ceilings. Not a flaw to be seen."

"Well, good."

"Next you need to choose your hall flooring."

"Yes, Nandina. Gil showed me the samples. I voted for Maple Syrup."

"You voted for Warm Honey. But how will you know what Warm Honey looks like in your actual hall, when you're sitting on the couch in my living room?"

"Okay, *you* go," I told her, "since you seem to feel so strongly about it."

She went. She came back to announce that Warm Honey was all right, she supposed, but in her opinion Butterscotch would work better.

I said, "Fine. Butterscotch it is."

I expected that to settle things, but somehow she didn't look satisfied.

In the middle of the slack period between Christmas and Easter, Charles proposed a new marketing ploy. "Gift season's coming up," he said. "Mother's Day, Father's Day, graduation, June weddings . . . What do you say we offer a collection of *Beginner's* books, slipcased together according to theme. For instance, wedding couples could get *The Beginner's Kitchen Equipment, The Beginner's Menu Plan,* and *The Beginner's Dinner Party.* No new publications involved; just existing ones, repackaged in a single color. I see high-gloss white for the wedding couples. Pink for Mother's Day, maybe. Are you all with me here?"

Nandina said, "Could you not have brought this up in this morning's meeting, Charles?" It was late afternoon, and we were all in the outer office. Nandina was leaving early again. She had her coat draped over one arm. But Charles tipped comfortably back in his chair and said, "This morning I hadn't thought of it yet. I thought of it over lunch. That always happens to me when I have a martini at lunch. I really ought to drink more."

Nandina rolled her eyes, and Irene laughed without looking up from the catalogue she was studying. But I said, "I see your point."

"It can't be just *any* martini, though," he told me. "I favor the ones at Montague's. They seem to have special powers."

"I mean about the boxed sets," I said. It had been a slow day, and I'd killed some time rearranging the *Beginner's* series by title rather than date. All the subjects were fresh in my mind. I said, "For the college graduates, say, we could have *Job Application, House Hunt,* and *Monthly Budget.* Maybe *Kitchen Equipment* in that set as well."

"Exactly," Charles said. "And we could easily update any of the older titles that needed it."

Peggy said, "But a slipcase is so limiting! Someone graduating from college might not be ready to buy a house yet. Or a bride might have bought *Monthly Budget* back when she first left home."

"That's the beauty of it," Charles told her. "People like complete sets. It fulfills some kind of collector's instinct. They'll buy a book all over again if it's changed color to match the others in a unit. Or they'll say, 'I'm sure *eventually* I'll be needing to house-hunt.'"

"You're right," Irene said. She set her catalogue down, one long scarlet fingernail marking her place. She said, "I just bought a brand-new boxed set of *Anne of Green Gables,* even though I already own most of it in various editions."

"*You* read *Anne of Green Gables?*" I asked her.

Peggy said, "Oh! That's true! I did the exact same thing with the *Winnie-the-Pooh* books."

Somehow, that was easier to visualize than Irene's curling up with *Anne of Green Gables.*

Only Nandina seemed unconvinced. "We'll talk about it tomorrow," she said as she headed for the door. "I'm late for an appointment."

"It's an idea, though, don't you think?" Charles called after her. And then to the rest of us, since Nandina was already gone, "Don't you think?"

"I do," Irene told him. "It's actually a brilliant idea."

"Oh, just *Beginner's Marketing,*" he said modestly.

"*Beginner's Flimflam,* is more like it," I told him.

"Hey! You said yourself that you saw my point."

"Well, yes," I said.

I was probably a bit jealous. Irene never said any of *my* ideas were brilliant.

I had one more commitment that day before I could leave: a meeting in my office with a Mr. Dupont, who wanted to publish his travel memoirs. The title of his book was *Contents May Have Shifted During Flight,* which I found promising, but the manuscript itself—at least as near as I could tell from leafing through it while he sat there—consisted of the usual eat-your-heart-out descriptions of breathtaking mountain views he had seen and delicious native dishes he had eaten. None of *my* concern, of course. We discussed costs, publication schedule, et cetera, and then I told him I was looking forward to doing business with him, and we stood up and shook hands and he left.

Peggy was the only one remaining in the outer office. She sat with her back to me, typing, and I was about to stop and make some friendly remark about how she shouldn't work too late when she said, still clicking away, "Don't forget your cane."

That irritated me, so I didn't stop after all. I said, "Got it," and walked past her to the coat tree, where I had hung my cane that morning.

"Twice last week you went home without it," she said.

"Yes? And? You admit I somehow managed to hobble back in the next day, even so."

Behind me, the computer keys went silent. I turned to find her looking at me with her very wide, very blue eyes.

"Oh," she said. "Are we supposed to pretend you don't *use* a cane?"

"No, I . . . It's just that in actual fact I actually don't really need it," I said. "I could do without it altogether if I had to."

"Oh."

I felt sort of bad about barking at her, but by that time she had gone back to her typing and so I just said, "Good night, then."

"Night," she said, without looking up.

It hadn't escaped my notice that I was very snappish these days. I thought about it as I was driving home. At our office meeting that morning, when Nandina brought us to order by tapping her pen against her coffee mug, I had nearly bitten her head off. "For God's sake, Nan," I had said, "do you have to act as if this were the Continental Congress?" But Nandina, after all, could give as good as she got. ("Yes, I do have to," she'd said, "and you know perfectly well that I hate to be called 'Nan.'") Peggy, on the other hand . . . A child might have drawn those eyes of hers, with the lashes rayed around them like sunbeams.

I parked in front of Nandina's and thought, *I'm turning into one of those grouches that kids are scared to visit on Halloween.*

Nandina's car was in the driveway, I was sorry to see. I had hoped she wouldn't be back from her appointment yet. I sighed and heaved myself out from behind the wheel. Maybe I could head straight upstairs to my room—bypass her entirely.

But when I opened the front door, I heard her talking in the kitchen. Evidently her appointment was here at the house; some workman, perhaps. And then the workman answered her and it was Gil. I recognized his voice even if I couldn't catch the words. Still in my jacket, I went out to the kitchen. "Hello?" I said.

Gil was sitting at the table, with his parka draped over his chair back and the sleeves of his flannel shirt rolled up. Nandina stood at the counter, slicing an orange. "Aaron!" she said, turning. "I didn't hear you come in."

"Hi, Gil," I said, and he raised one baseball-mitt hand and said, "How you doing, Aaron."

"Everything okay at the house?" I asked. He didn't usually come by till later in the evening.

But he said, "Oh, yes," and then started patting his shirt pockets. "I did bring that lighting estimate," he said. "*Somewhere here . . .*"

"I'm making Gil a drink," Nandina told me. "Would you care for one?"

"What's in it?"

"Orange juice, a kiwi, ginger root, a papaya—"

"Wow."

"—half a cantaloupe, two stalks of celery . . ."

She had her juice extractor out on the counter—a complicated piece of equipment I hadn't seen in use since that time a few years back when she was dating a vegan. It had turned out to be a lot of work, as I recalled. Supposedly you could clean the thing in the dishwasher, but that wasn't very practical, since the various parts constituted an entire load in themselves.

Wait.

When she was dating a . . .

I looked from her to Gil, who was sitting there placidly waiting for his drink. I looked again at Nandina.

She blushed.

I said, "Oh."

5

How could I have missed so many clues?

Nandina's frequent intrusions on my meetings with Gil, for instance. Granted, she had always been a bit nosy, but this was extreme: if Gil and I were conferring in the living room, she just happened to need a book from the living-room bookcase, and then, while she was at it, she had to offer us some refreshments, and when she returned with a tray, she would oh-so-casually linger to contribute her two bits, eventually drifting toward a chair and dropping into it as if without realizing what she was doing.

And her willingness to drive over to my house on the slightest excuse—to empty my fridge, check on the plastering, verify my choice of caramel or whatever-it-was flooring. Always in the daytime, you notice. Always when Gil was most likely to be there as well.

And those questions she had asked about his background. Why, she hadn't been asking out of suspicion! That was personal curiosity. She was like a high-school girl who ferrets out the most trivial details about a boy she has a crush on—his gym schedule and his homeroom number. And, exactly like a high-school girl, she seized on every opportunity to speak his name. "Gilead," she had said, and her spoon had halted in the saucepan.

Plus, she never changed into a housecoat anymore. I hadn't seen her in a housecoat in weeks.

But did Gil return her affections?

I felt a twinge that was almost a pain. I couldn't bear it if I were forced to pity her.

Consider this, though: Gil really hadn't needed to meet with me as often as he did. More than once I had told him that the work appeared to be going fine, and he should just let me know the next time he had any issues to discuss. It seemed he constantly had issues. And at every meeting he was more talkative; more extraneous subjects arose; it seemed more like a conversation with a friend. Here I'd been flattering myself that it was me he was warming to! I'd sniffed the air when he'd walked in recently, caught the scent of Old Spice, and said, "*Somebody's* got plans for the evening," expecting we might embark on a little chitchat about his social life. But he had merely turned red, and I had wondered if I'd overstepped—assumed too quickly that we were more than employer-employee.

Besides which, how come he had told her, but not me, that he'd be coming unusually early that evening?

I didn't say anything direct to either one of them. I accepted a glass of Nandina's juice, sat talking with them a few minutes, let Gil present his report on that day's work. But underneath, I was extremely alert, and I saw how Nandina continued to hang around even though his report concerned some antiquated wiring they'd discovered in my living-room wall—*not* an interesting topic, and certainly not one that called for her opinion. I saw how their hands happened to brush when he passed her his empty glass. How she leaned against the doorframe and tipped her head alluringly as we were seeing him out at the end of the meeting.

Then she hurried back to the kitchen to start supper preparations, not giving me so much as a glance, allowing me no chance to question her.

I didn't pursue it, of course. She was a fully grown woman. She had a right to her privacy.

Everything I knew about Gil so far had made me like him. He seemed to be a good man—honest, reliable, skilled, kindhearted. He may not have finished college, but he was clearly intelligent, and I imagined that he and Nandina could operate on a more or less equal footing. So I had no objections.

But I couldn't help feeling, oh, a bit wistful as I watched them together over the next couple of weeks.

It was April, by then—early spring. Although the weather was still coolish, the daffodils were in full bloom and the trees were starting to flower. Gil and Nandina began to go out openly on what I guess you might call dates. The first date, shortly after the juicer episode, Nandina informed me about obliquely by announcing that she wouldn't be cooking supper the following evening. Gil had suggested they try this new café in Hampden, she said. I said, "Oh, okay, maybe I'll reheat some of that beef stew"—as if food were really the issue here. The next evening, I sat reading the newspaper on the couch, and when Gil rang the doorbell I let Nandina answer. He stepped into the living room to say, "Hey there, Aaron," and I raised my head and said, "How you doing, Gil." He looked sheepish but determined, his face gleaming from a recent shave and his short-sleeved shirt carefully pressed. How long had he been coming to this house in clothes too fresh to have been that day's work clothes? Almost from the start of our dealings together, I realized. So he may have felt attracted to Nandina all along.

I was genuinely glad for them, I swear. And yet, after they had taken their leave, when I turned in my seat to watch them through the front window, I felt stabbed to the heart by the sight of their two figures walking side by side toward Gil's pickup. They were almost touching but not quite; there was perhaps an inch or two of empty space between them, and you could tell somehow that both of them were very conscious of this space—acutely conscious, *electrically* conscious. I thought of a moment early in my acquaintance with Dorothy, when she had offered to show me around her workplace. She stood up and went to her office door, and I jumped to my feet to follow, reaching past her and over her head to pull the door farther open. I guess it must have confused her. She stepped back. For an instant she was standing under the shelter of my arm, and although there was not one single point of contact between us, I felt I was surrounding her with an invisible layer of warmth and protection.

Even that early, I loved her.

We met in March of 1996, during *The Beginner's Cancer*. Byron Worth, M.D., was our writer—an internist who had already supplied the material for *The Beginner's Childbirth* and *The Beginner's Heart Attack*. These books were not particularly technical, you understand. They were more on the order of household-hint collections: how to sleep comfortably in the advanced stages of pregnancy, how to order heart-healthfully in restaurants. For the cancer book Dr. Worth had already turned in the chemo section, which included some delicious-sounding recipes for calorie-rich smoothies, but in radiology he fell short, by his own admission. He said we probably needed to consult a specialist. And that's how I came to make an appointment with Dr. Dorothy Rosales, who had treated Charles's father-in-law after his thyroid surgery.

She was wearing a white coat so crisp that it could have stood on its own, but her trousers were creased and rumpled, in part because they were too long for her. They buckled over the insteps of her cloddish shoes and they trailed the ground at her heels. This made her seem even shorter than she actually was, and wider. She was standing by a bookshelf when her receptionist showed me into her office. She was consulting some large, thick volume, and since her glasses were meant for distance she had pushed them up onto her forehead, which gave her a peculiar, quadruple-eyed aspect that caused me to start grinning the instant I saw her. But even in that first glance, I liked her broad, tan face and her tranquil expression. I congratulated myself for perceiving that her unbecomingly chopped hair was—as they say—as black as a raven's wing.

I said, "Dr. Rosales?"

"Yes."

"I'm Aaron Woolcott. I called you about consulting on our book project."

"Yes, I know," she said.

This threw me off my stride for a moment. I hesitated, and then I held out my hand. "It's good to meet you," I said.

Her own hand was warm and cushioned but rough-skinned. She shook mine efficiently and then stepped back to lower her glasses to their proper position. "What's wrong with your arm?" she asked me.

It's true that when I extend my arm to shake hands, I tend to aid it slightly by supporting my elbow with my good hand. But most people don't catch that, or at least if they do they don't comment. I said, "Oh, just a childhood illness."

"Huh," she said. "Well, have a seat."

I sat down in a molded plastic chair in front of her desk. There was another chair next to it. I imagined that two people generally came for the initial consultation—a married couple, or a grown son or daughter with an aged parent. This office must have seen some very distraught visitors. But Dr. Rosales, settling behind her desk now in a deliberate, unhurried way, would have made them feel instantly reassured. She placed her palms together and said, "I'm not certain what you want of me."

"Well, no actual writing," I told her. "We have an internist doing that for us, Dr. Byron Worth."

I paused, giving her time to react if she recognized the name. Instead, she just went on watching me. Her eyes were pure black through and through, without a hint of any other colors behind them. For the first time it crossed my mind that she might be a foreigner; I mean more foreign than a mere descendant of someone Hispanic.

"Dr. Worth is trying to give our readers a few tips for handling the day-to-day obstacles confronted by the cancer patient," I said.

"He's discussed the emotional issues, the doctor-patient trans-actions, the practical aspects of various treatment options . . . except for radiation, which he hasn't had any experience with. He suggested that an oncology radiologist might walk us through that—tell us what the patient can expect, in the most concrete terms."

"I see," she said.

Silence.

"Of course we would pay you for your time, and acknowledge your assistance in the preface."

I considered going on to tell her that, after *The Beginner's Childbirth,* a doula who'd been mentioned by name had tripled her client load. But I wasn't sure that physicians actively sought out business in quite the same way. Especially this physician. She seemed to need nothing. She seemed entire in herself.

She seemed fascinating.

"Say," I said. "It's almost noon. May I take you out to lunch so that we can discuss this further?"

"I'm not hungry," she said.

"Uh . . ."

"What," she said, "you just want to know the process? But the process is different for each type of tumor. For each individual patient, even."

"Oh, well, we wouldn't have to go into great detail," I told her. "Nothing excessively medical, ha ha."

I was acting like an idiot. Dr. Rosales was sitting back and watching me. I started racking my brain for some sample ques-tions, but none came to mind. Supposedly I was there just to make the arrangements. Then Dr. Worth would take over.

No way was I going to let him take over Dorothy Rosales.

"All right," I said, "here's a plan. I will make up a written list this very afternoon of what we need to know. Then, before you decide either way, you could look through it. Maybe over dinner; I could buy you dinner. Unless . . . you have a husband to get home to?"

"No."

"Dinner at the Old Bay," I said. I had to struggle to keep the happiness out of my voice. I'd already noticed that she wasn't wearing a wedding ring, but nowadays that didn't mean much. "As soon as you get off work tonight."

"I don't understand," she said. "Why does this have to involve food?"

"Well . . . you'd need to eat anyway, right?"

"Right," she said, and she looked relieved. I could tell this was the kind of logic that appealed to her. "Fine, Mr.—"

"Woolcott. Aaron."

"Where is this Old Bay place?"

"Oh, I can drive you there. I'll swing by and pick you up."

"Never mind," she said. "Our lot has a punch-clock."

"Excuse me?"

"Our parking lot. We pay by the hour. No point forking over any more money than I have to."

"Oh."

She stood up, and I stood, too. "I won't be finished here till seven," she told me.

"That's okay! I'll reserve a table for half past. The restaurant is only about fifteen minutes from here."

"In that case, a quarter past would appear to be more appropriate," she said.

"Fine," I said. "A quarter past."

I took a business card from my billfold and wrote down the Old Bay's address. As a rule I would have written it on the blank side of the card, but this time I chose the front. I wanted her to become familiar with my name. I wanted her to start calling me "Aaron."

But all she said when we parted was, "Goodbye, then." She didn't use any form of my name. And she didn't bother seeing me out.

I could tell she must not be from Baltimore, because anyone from Baltimore would have known the Old Bay. That was where all our parents used to eat. It was old-fashioned in both good ways and bad. (The crab soup, for instance, was the real thing, but the waiters were in their eighties and the atmosphere was gloomy and dank.) I had chosen it for geographical reasons, since it wasn't far from Dorothy's office, but also I wanted a place that was not too businesslike, not too efficient. I wanted her to start thinking of me in a more, so to speak, social light.

Well. Clearly I had my work cut out for me, because she arrived in her doctor coat. Dressed-up couples dotted the room, the women in the soft pastels of early spring, but there stood Dorothy beside the maître d' with her leather satchel slung bandolier-style across her chest and her hands thrust deep in the pockets of her starched white coat.

I stood up and raised a hand. She headed for my table, leaving the maître d' in her dust. "Hi," she said when she reached me. She took hold of the chair opposite mine, but I beat her to it and slid it out for her. "Welcome!" I told her as she sat down. I returned to my own chair. "Thank—thank you for coming."

"It's awfully dark," she said, looking around the room. She freed herself from her satchel and set it at her feet. "You're expecting me to read in this?"

"Read? Oh, no, only the menu," I said, and I gave a chuckle that came out sounding fake. "I did phone Dr. Worth for a list of questions to ask you, but he said what he would prefer is, we should arrange a time when you can walk me through your facility. See the process from start to finish, as if I were a patient."

In fact, I had not mentioned a word of this to Dr. Worth, but I doubted if he would object to my doing some of his research for him.

Dorothy said, "So . . . we came to this restaurant just to set up an appointment?"

"But then also we need to discuss your terms. How much would you propose to be paid, for one thing, and—what would you like to drink?"

Our waiter had arrived, was why I asked, but Dorothy looked startled, perhaps imagining for an instant that this was another business decision. Then her expression cleared, and she told the waiter, "A Diet Pepsi, please."

"Diet!" I said. "A doctor, drinking artificial sweeteners?"

She blinked.

"Don't you know what aspartame does to your central nervous system?" I asked. (I'd been heavily influenced by *The Beginner's Book of Nutrition,* not to mention my sister's anti-soft-drink crusade.) "Have a glass of wine, instead. A red wine; good for your heart."

"Well . . . all right."

I accepted the wine list from the waiter and chose a Malbec, two glasses. When the waiter had left, Dorothy said, "I'm not very used to drinking alcohol."

"But you're familiar with the virtues of the Mediterranean diet, surely."

"Yes," she said. Her eyes narrowed.

"And I know you must have heard about olive oil."

"Look," she said. "Are you going to start telling me your symptoms?"

"What?"

"I'm here to discuss a book project, okay? I don't want to check out some little freckle that might be cancer."

"Check out *what*? What freckle?"

"Or hear about some time when you thought your pulse might have skipped a beat."

"Are you out of your mind?" I asked.

She started looking uncertain.

"My pulse is perfect!" I said. "What are you talking about?"

"Sorry," she said.

She lowered her gaze to her place setting. She moved her spoon half an inch to her right. She said, "A lot of times, people outside of the office ask me for free advice. Even if they're just sitting next to me on an airplane, they ask."

"Did *I* ask? Did you hear me ask you anything?"

"Well, but I thought—"

"You seem to be suffering from a serious misapprehension," I told her. "If I need advice, I'll make an appointment with my family physician. Who is excellent, by the way, and knows my entire medical history besides, not that I ever have the slightest reason to call on him."

"I already said I was sorry."

She took off her glasses and polished them on her napkin, still keeping her eyes lowered. Her eyelashes were thick but very short and stubby. Her mouth was clamped in a thin, unhappy line.

I said, "Hey. Dorothy. Want to start over?"

There was a pause. I saw the corners of her lips start to twitch, and then she looked up at me and smiled.

It makes me sad now to think back on the early days of our courtship. We didn't know anything at all. Dorothy didn't even know it *was* a courtship, at the beginning, and I was kind of like an overgrown puppy, at least as I picture myself from this distance. I was romping around her all eager and panting, dying to impress her, while for some time she remained stolidly oblivious.

By that stage of life, I'd had my fair share of romances. I had left behind the high-school girls who were so fearful of seeming freakish themselves that they couldn't afford to be seen with me, and in college I became a kind of pet project for the aspiring social workers that all the young women of college age seemed to be. They associated my cane with, who knows, old war wounds or something. They took the premature glints of white in my hair as a sign of mysterious past sufferings. As you might surmise, I had an allergy to this viewpoint, but usually at the outset I didn't suspect that they held it. (Or didn't let myself suspect.) I just gave myself over to what I fancied was true love. As soon as I grasped the situation, though, I would walk out. Or sometimes *they* would walk out, once they lost all hope of rescuing me. Then I graduated, and in the year and a half since, I had pretty much stuck to myself, taking care to avoid the various sweet young women that my family seemed to keep strewing in my path.

You see now why I found Dorothy so appealing—Dorothy, who wouldn't even discuss the Mediterranean diet with me.

I went to her office a few days later to tour her treatment rooms, asking what if a patient had this kind of tumor, what if a patient had that kind of tumor. I went again with a list of follow-up questions that Dr. Worth had supposedly dictated to me. And after that, of course, I had to show her my rough draft over another dinner, this time at a place with better lighting.

Then a major development: I suggested we go to a movie the following evening. An outing with no useful purpose. She had a little trouble with that one. I saw her working to make the adjustment in her mind—switching me from "business" to "pleasure." She said, "I don't know," and then she said, "What movie were you thinking of?"

"Whichever one you like," I told her. "I would let you choose."

"Well," she said. "Okay. I don't have anything better to do."

We went to the movie—a documentary, as I recall—and then, a few days later, we went to another one, and after that to a couple more meals. We talked about her work, and my work, and the news on TV, and the books we were reading. (She read seriously and pragmatically, always about something scientific if not specifically radiological.) We traded the usual growing-up stories. She hadn't been back to see her family in years, she said. She seemed amused to hear that I lived in an apartment only blocks away from my parents.

At that first movie I took her elbow to usher her into her seat, and at the second I sat with my shoulder touching hers. Leaning across the table to make a point to her over dinner, I covered her hand with mine; parting at the end of each evening, I began giving her a brief hug—but no more of a hug than I might give a friend. Oh, I was cagey, all right. I didn't completely understand her; I couldn't read her feelings. And already I knew that this was too important for me to risk any missteps.

In April I brought her a copy of *The Beginner's Income Tax*, which was not really about taxes but about organizing receipts and such. She was hopelessly disorganized, she claimed; and then, as if to prove it, she forgot to take the book with her when we left the restaurant. I worried about what this meant. I felt she had forgotten *me*—easy come, easy go, she was saying—and it didn't help that when I offered to turn the car around that minute and go retrieve it, she said never mind, she would just phone the restaurant later.

Did she care about me even a little?

Then she asked why I didn't have a handicapped license plate. We were walking toward my car at the time; we'd been to the Everyman Theatre. I said, "Because I don't need a handicapped license plate."

"You're bound to throw your back out of whack, walking the distances you do with that limp. I'm surprised it hasn't already happened."

I said nothing.

"Would you like me to fill in a form for the Motor Vehicle people?"

"No, thanks," I said.

"Or maybe you'd prefer a hang-tag. Then we could switch it to my car if I were the one driving."

"I told you, no," I said.

She fell silent. We got into the car and I drove her home. By this time I knew where she lived—a basement apartment down near the old stadium—but I hadn't been inside, and I had planned to suggest that evening that I come in with her. I didn't, though. I said, "Well, good night," and I reached across her to open her door.

She looked at me for a moment, and then she said, "Thank you, Aaron," and got out. I waited till she was safely in her building and then I drove away. I was feeling kind of depressed, to be honest. I don't mean I'd fallen out of love with her or anything like that, but I felt very low, all at once. Very tired. I felt weary to the bone.

Pursuing the theme of let's-see-each-other's-apartments, I had planned next to invite her to supper at my place. I was thinking I would fix her my famous spaghetti and meatballs. But now I put that off a few days, because it seemed like so much trouble. I would have to get that special mix of different ground meats, for one thing. Veal and so on. Pork. I didn't trust an ordinary supermarket for that; I'd have to go to the butcher. It seemed a huge amount of effort for a dish that was really, when you came down to it, not all that distinctive.

I gave it a rest. I told myself I needed some space. Good grief, we'd gone out six evenings in the past two weeks—one time, twice in a row.

She telephoned me on Wednesday. (We'd last seen each other on Saturday.) She didn't have my number and so she called Woolcott Publishing, and Peggy stuck her head in my door and said, "Dr. Rosales? On Line Two?"

She could have just buzzed me, but clearly she was wondering what a doctor could be calling me for. I refused to satisfy her curiosity. "Thanks," was all I told her, and I waited till she was gone before I picked up the receiver.

"Hello," I said.

"Hi, Aaron, it's Dorothy."

"Hello, Dorothy."

"I haven't heard from you in a while."

This was more direct than I was comfortable with. I felt partly taken aback and partly, I have to say, admiring. Wasn't it just like her!

"I've been busy," I told her.

"Oh."

"A lot of work piling up."

"Well, I'd like to invite you to supper," she said.

"Supper?"

"I would cook."

"Oh!"

I don't know why this was so unexpected. Somehow, I just couldn't picture Dorothy cooking. But *trying* to picture it made me see her hands, which were very smooth across the backs in spite of her raspy fingers, and golden-brown and chubby. I was swept with a wave of longing. I said, "I'd love to come to supper."

"Good. Shall we say eight o'clock?"

"Tonight?"

"Eight tonight."

"I'll be there," I said.

Later—much later, when we were making our wedding plans—Dorothy told me all that had gone into that supper invitation. She began with her reason for issuing it: how she'd grown aware, in the four days when I didn't call, of the extreme quiet and solitude of her existence. "I saw that I had no close friends, no family life; and at work they were always complaining about my failure to 'interact,' whatever that means. . . ." She described how she'd rearranged her apartment before my arrival, frantically shoving furniture every which way and stuffing books and papers and cast-off clothes into closets, into bureau drawers, wherever they would fit; and how she'd racked her brains over the menu. "All men like steak, right? So I called the Pratt Library's reference section to see how to cook a steak. They suggested grilling or broiling, but I didn't own a grill and I wasn't all that clear about broiling, so they said okay, fry it in a pan. . . . And then the peas, well, that was no problem; everybody knows how to cook a box of peas. . . ."

But did she give the same amount of forethought to what we would talk about?

Oh, probably not. Probably that was just happenstance. After all, it was I who started things, when I commented on the size of her apartment. "This place is huge," I said when I walked in. It was shabby but sprawling, with an actual dining room opening off the living room. "How many bedrooms do you have?"

"Three," she told me.

"Three! All for one person!"

"Well, I used to have a roommate, but he moved."

"Ah."

I accepted the seat she offered me, at the end of a jangling metal daybed covered with an Indian spread. On the coffee table she had already set out wineglasses and a bottle of wine (Malbec, I saw), and she handed me the bottle along with a corkscrew. Then she sat down next to me. This close, I could smell her perfume, or her shampoo or something. She was wearing a scoop-necked black knit top I hadn't seen before, along with her usual black trousers. I wondered if this was her version of dressing up.

It seemed her mind was still on her roommate. She said, "He moved because I wasn't . . . doctorly enough."

"Doctorly."

"For instance, one time he said, 'Everything I eat tastes too salty. Why do you think that could be?' I said, 'I have no idea.' He said, 'No, really: why?' 'Maybe it *is* too salty,' I said. He said, 'No, other people don't think so. Is there anything that could be a symptom of?' I said, 'Well, dehydration, maybe. Or a brain tumor.' 'Brain tumor!' he said. 'Oh, my God!'"

I missed her point at first. She stopped speaking and looked at me expectantly, and I said, "What an idiot."

"He would ask me to palpate a swollen gland," she said after a pause, "or he'd wonder what his backache meant, a perfectly normal backache he got from lifting weights, or he'd want me to write a prescription for his migraines."

"Well, that's ridiculous!" I said. "He was your roommate, not your patient."

Another pause. Then she said, "Actually, he was more like a . . . We were more like a couple, actually."

This shouldn't have come as a shock. She was a woman in her thirties; you would wonder what was wrong with her if there'd never been a man in her life. But somehow I had flattered myself that I was the very first one to appreciate her properly. I said, "You were a *serious* couple?"

She was following her own tack. She said, "I see now that he probably thought I wasn't enough of a . . . caregiver."

"Ridiculous," I said again.

"So I said to myself, 'I have to learn from that experience.'"

She still wore her expectant look.

This time, I got it.

I said, "Oh."

"I wouldn't want a person to think that I'm not . . . concerned."

I said, "Oh, sweetheart. Dearest heart. I would never need you to be concerned for *me*."

And I cupped her face and leaned forward to kiss her, and she kissed me back.

I could tell that people found Dorothy an unexpected choice.

My father said she was "interesting"—the same word he used when he was confronted with one of my mother's more experimental casseroles.

My mother asked how old she was.

"I haven't the slightest idea," I said.

(In fact, Dorothy was thirty-two. I was twenty-four and a half.)

"It's only," my mother said, "that I was thinking Danika Jones would have been closer to your own age."

"Who?"

"Danika at work, Aaron. What do you mean, 'Who?'"

Danika was our designer, the designer preceding Irene. My father had hired her as his final act before handing over the business, and all at once I thought I saw why. I said, "Danika! She wears toenail polish!"

"What's wrong with that?" my mother asked.

"I always feel uneasy about women who polish their toenails. It makes me wonder what they're hiding."

"Oh, Aaron," my mother said sadly. "When will you under-stand how attractive you are? You could have any girl you wanted; someday you're going to realize that."

My sister said Dorothy was okay, she guessed, if you didn't mind a woman with the social skills of a panda bear. That just made me laugh. Dorothy *was* a bit like a panda bear. She had that same roundness and compactness, that same staunch way of carrying herself.

Only I knew that underneath her boxy clothes, she was the shape of a little clay urn. Her skin had a burnished olive glow, and there was a kind of calm to her, a lit-from-within calm, that made me feel at rest whenever I was with her.

We were married in my family's church, but just in the min-ister's private office, with my parents and my sister as witnesses. Surprisingly, Dorothy had told me that it would be all right with her if I wanted something fancier, but of course I didn't. The sim-pler the better, I felt. Simple and straightforward. And we didn't take a honeymoon, because of Dorothy's work schedule. We just went back to our normal lives.

It was early July when we married. We had known each other four months.

My cousin Roger once told me, on the eve of his third wedding, that he felt marriage was addictive. Then he corrected himself. "I mean *early* marriage," he said. "The very start of a marriage. It's like a whole new beginning. You're entirely brand-new people; you haven't made any mistakes yet. You have a new place to live and new dishes and this new kind of, like, identity, this 'we' that gets invited everywhere together now. Why, sometimes your wife will have a brand-new name, even."

Dorothy still had her old name, and we were living temporarily in my old apartment, but in all other respects, what he said was true. Everything we did together in our new life was a first-time event, as if we had been reborn. On weekends, especially, when we didn't go to work, I felt almost shiny, almost wet behind the ears, as we ventured forth upon the day. We ate breakfast together, we went to the supermarket together, we discussed whether we could afford to buy a house together. Could this really be me? Gimpy, geeky Aaron, acting like a regular husband?

And if I was surprised by myself, I was surprised even more by Dorothy. That she would consent to go shopping for something so prosaic as a vacuum cleaner, for instance—that she deigned to consider the merits of canister over upright—came as a revelation. As did the fact that she made a point of using the phrase "my husband" when speaking to strangers. "My husband thinks our vacuum should have a hypoallergenic filter." That tickled me no end.

Also, she turned out to be a cuddler. Who would ever have guessed? She stayed nestled within the scoop of my body all night long, although you might suppose she'd be the brisk type once the sex was over. She kept close to me in crowds, often taking my hand surreptitiously as I stood talking with someone. I would feel those rough, pudgy fingers slipping stealthily between mine and I would have to struggle not to break into a smile.

I'm not saying that we didn't encounter a few little bumps in the road. Every couple has to make some adjustments, isn't that so? Especially when they've been accustomed to living on their own. Oh, we experienced our fair share of misunderstandings and crossed signals and faulty timing. On any number of occasions, we disappointed each other.

For one thing, I hadn't completely comprehended before that Dorothy had zero interest in food. Zero. Not only did she almost never cook, which was fine with me, but she failed to appreciate what *I* cooked, which wasn't fine at all. She would arrive at the table with a sheaf of mail that she opened and read between mouthfuls. "What do you think of the fish?" I would ask her, and she would say, "Hmm? Oh. It's good," without lifting her eyes from the letter she was reading.

And she lacked sufficient respect for physical objects. She gave no thought to their assigned places, to their maintenance and upkeep. She didn't—how can I put it? She didn't properly value things.

If she had properly valued *me,* for instance, wouldn't she have taken more care with her appearance? It was true that I had been charmed at first by her lack of vanity, but now and then it struck me that she was looking almost, well, plain, and that this plainness seemed willful. As the months went by I found myself noticing more and more her clumsy clothes, her aggressively plodding walk, her tendency to leave her hair unwashed one day too long.

And Dorothy, for her part, seemed to find me unreasonably prickly. She'd say, "You'll probably bite my head off, but . . . ," and then she'd finish with something innocuous, such as an offer to take a turn driving when we were on a long car trip. I'd say, "Why would you think that, Dorothy? Why would I bite your head off?" But unintentionally, I would be using a biting-her-head-off tone as I asked, because it irritated me when she tiptoed around my feelings that way. So, in fact, I'd proved her right. I could see it in her expression, although she would carefully not say so. And I would observe her not saying so, and I would feel all the more irritated.

It kills me now to remember these things.

I felt she expected something of me that she wouldn't state outright. Her face would fall for no reason sometimes, and I would say, "What? What is it?" but she would say it was nothing. I could sense that I had let her down, but I had no idea how.

Once, she had a conference in L.A., but she said that she was thinking she might skip it. She didn't like leaving me to manage on my own for so long, she said. (This was fairly early in our marriage.) I said, "Don't skip it for *my* sake," and she said, "Maybe you could come with me. Would you like that? They always have guided bus tours and such for the spouses during the day."

"Great," I said. "I could bring my knitting."

"Oh, why be that way? I only meant—"

"Dorothy," I said. "I was joking. Don't *worry* about me. It's not as if I depend on you to take care of me, after all."

I meant that as a statement of fact. It wasn't an accusation; who could read it as an accusation? But Dorothy did. I could tell by her face. She didn't say anything more, and she got a sort of closed look.

I *tried* to smooth things over. I said, "But thanks for your concern." It didn't do any good, though. She stayed quiet throughout the evening, and the next day she left for her conference and I missed her like some kind of, almost, organ out of my body, and I think she missed me, too, because she phoned me from Los Angeles several times a day and she'd say, "What are you doing right now?" and, "I really wish you were here." I wished I were there, too, and I couldn't believe I had wasted that chance to be with her. I made a lot of promises to myself about being more easygoing in the future, not so quick to take umbrage, but then, when she came home, the very first thing she did was get mad at me about this thorn I had in my index finger. I'm serious. While she was gone I had cut back the barberry bush that was poking over the railing of our rear balcony, and you know how barberry thorns are so microscopic and so hard to get out. I figured it would just work its own way out, but it hadn't yet, and my finger had started swelling and turning red. She said, "What *is* this? This is infected!"

"Yes, I think it must be," I said.

"What is the *matter* with you?"

"Nothing's the matter with me," I said. "I have a thorn in my finger, okay? Sooner or later I'll see this little black speck emerging and I'll yank it. Any objections?"

"Yank it with what?" she asked.

"Tweezers, of course."

"Yank it with what *hand,* Aaron? It's in your left index finger. How are you going to work a pair of tweezers with your right hand?"

"I can do that," I told her.

"You cannot. You should have asked someone for help. Instead you just . . . sat here, just sat here for a week, waiting for me to come home so I'd have to say, 'Oh, no, I'm so sorry, how could I have left you on your own to deal with this?' And everyone else would say, all your family and your office would say, 'Look at that: she wasn't even there to take his thorn out and now he has a major infection and maybe even will need an amputation, can you believe it?'"

"Amputation!" I said. "Are you *nuts*?"

But she just reached for the matchbox above the stove and went off to find a needle, and when she came back she leaned over my finger, her lips turned disapprovingly downward, my hand squeezed tightly in hers, and she pierced the skin one time and the thorn shot out like an arrow.

"There," she said crisply, and she dabbed the wound with disinfectant.

Then she bent her head and pressed her cheek against the back of my hand, and her skin felt as soft as petals.

Well, we survived these little glitches. We papered over them, we went on with our lives. It's true that we no longer had quite the same newborn shine, but nobody keeps that forever, right? The important thing was, we loved each other. All I had to do to remind myself of that was to cast my thoughts back to the moment we met. To my lonesome, unattached, unsuspecting self following the receptionist down the corridor of the Radiology Center. The receptionist comes to a stop and raps on a half-open door. Then she pushes it farther open, and I step through it, and Dorothy raises her eyes from her book. Our story begins.

I got up from Nandina's couch and looked around for my cane, which I finally found propped in a corner. I let myself out the front door; I locked it behind me; I set off down the sidewalk.

Left onto Clifton Lane, left again on Summit and down to Wyndhurst. Then south on Woodlawn a good long way until I reached Rumor Road. *My* road, only three blocks long and lined with flowering pear trees. It was twilight by now, but I could still hear birds singing. One bird was calling out, "*'Scuse* me! *'Scuse* me!" and insects were zipping away, keeping up that background clatter that you never really hear unless you stop to think about it.

I was developing a bit of an ache in the left side of my lower back, but that always happened when I walked any distance and I paid it no attention. I started walking even faster, because I knew that beyond the slight bend up ahead I would catch my first sight of our house. The bend was marked by a single tree of a different type from the others; I didn't know the name. This tree bore huge pink, floppy flowers, and they were so abundant this year that I drew a deep breath as I approached it, expecting a strong perfume. I couldn't detect one, though. Instead I smelled . . . Well, it was something like isopropyl alcohol, the faintest, most delicate scent of alcohol floating on the breeze, mixed with plain Ivory soap. The exact scent of my wife.

Then I rounded the bend, and I saw her standing on the sidewalk.

She was some ten feet away from me, facing our house and gazing at it, but when she heard my footsteps she turned in my direction. She was wearing her wide black trousers and a gray shirt. Both were the kind of colors that blended into the fading light, and yet she herself was absolutely solid—as solid as you or I, and in fact almost more so, in some odd way; solid and sturdy and opaque. I had forgotten that rebellious little quirk of black hair that stood up from the crown of her head. I'd forgotten how she always stood tipping a bit backward, ducklike, on her heels.

She watched me intently as I came nearer, with her chin

slightly raised and her eyes fixed on mine. I arrived in front of her. I drew in a deep breath. I thought I would never in all my life smell a more wonderful combination than isopropyl alcohol and plain soap.

"Dorothy," I said.

I'm not sure if I spoke aloud. I have a feeling I may have just thought it, in the very depths of my being.

I said, "Dorothy, my dear one. My only, only Dorothy."

"Hello, Aaron," she said.

She looked into my face for a moment, and then she turned and walked away. But I didn't feel she was abandoning me. I knew, somehow, that she had stayed as long right then as she was able and that she would come again as soon as she could. So I stood still and watched her leave without attempting to follow. I watched her reach the end of the block, take a right on Hawthorn, and vanish.

Then I turned and started back to Nandina's. I hadn't so much as glanced at our house. What did I care about our house? I walked in a kind of trance, keeping my gait as nearly level as possible, as if Dorothy had been a liquid and now I was brimful of her and moving slowly and gently so as not to spill over.

6

I waited. I waited.

For days on end I stayed suspended, waiting for her to come back.

Since our street was where she had shown up, I figured that was where she would be most likely to show up again. In fact, I kicked myself for not going there before now. Had she been wandering Rumor Road all these months, wondering where I was? I could hardly bear to think about all my lost opportunities.

It turned out that in the daytime our little house was Grand Central Station. Workmen came and went; power tools whizzed and hammers pounded. I was lost in all the confusion; nobody knew who I was. When I peered in through the screen at my new Butterscotch floor, a guy in a bandanna head-wrap asked if I had some business there. But once I identified myself, they were all over me. Would I like to take a tour? Would I care to see the sunporch? Gil was not around at the time, but clearly these men knew my story. They spoke to me in the respectful tones of funeral guests. They made me feel elderly, although we were all more or less the same age.

I didn't really want a tour of the house, but I felt that I shouldn't say no. (I was bearing in mind Nandina's remark about how workmen needed to feel appreciated.) And after we got started, it wasn't as bad as I had feared. The guy in the head-wrap led the way, and the others, all five or six of them, dropped what they were doing to trail behind us. They were conspicuously silent at first, listening as the head-wrap guy explained what we were looking at. "Very nice," I murmured, and, "Mmhmm. I see." Then, bit by bit, they began to chime in, talking over each other, telling me how this particular molding had been the devil to find a match for, how they'd had to rip out that cornice three times before they got it right. "You guys are doing great," I told them, and they went into an "Aw, shucks" routine and stuck their hands in their rear pockets and looked down at their shoes.

I felt ashamed of myself for waiting so long to do this. Now my refusal to visit seemed petulant, like a child kicking his bicycle after it's tipped him over. What had happened wasn't the *house's* fault. And besides, these men had stripped away so much that it didn't seem like the same place anymore. Even my bedroom, which they hadn't touched, was unrecognizable, heaped as it was with a jumble of furniture shrouded in white canvas.

I felt all the more ashamed when Gil walked in. He looked so surprised to see me, and so pleased; he actually blushed, and then he had to take me around and show me everything I'd just seen.

So: a good visit, all in all. But what I learned from it was, no point going there during work hours if I hoped to catch sight of Dorothy again.

I took to stopping by in the evenings, therefore, or very early on Sunday mornings, when the neighbors weren't out and about yet. At 6:30 or 7 a.m. I would park out front and just sit a while, staring through the windshield at the spot where I had seen Dorothy. I would relive every detail of that encounter, the way you'd relive a dream that you were trying to sink back into. Her square gray shirt, her black trousers, the tilt of her chin as she watched me approach, the steadiness of her gaze. My eyes worked so hard to summon her up that they were practically *knitting* her, but even so, she failed to appear.

Then I'd get out of my car and walk toward the house. Very slowly, though, just in case she wanted to intercept me at any point. I would pause after every few steps and look around me in an elaborately interested way, up at the shards of blue sky showing through the trees, down at the sidewalk with its imprint of old leaf stains like patterned fabric. But she didn't appear, and so eventually I would unlock my front door, brace myself, and step inside.

The detritus of the workmen's daily lives—their drink cups and crumpled drop cloths and jar lids full of cigarette stubs—made the house feel populated even though it was empty. I would have to stand still a moment, regaining my sense of solitude. After that I would move through the house from front to back, from hallway to kitchen.

No Dorothy. Smells of fresh-cut lumber, cigarette smoke, damp plaster, but no soap or isopropyl alcohol. In the kitchen I would stand waiting so long that the silence began to echo at me like the silence inside a seashell, but she never said, "Hello, Aaron."

Had she said those words aloud? Or had they just been in my mind, the same way I'd told her my own thoughts? Had the whole *scene* been in my mind? Had I been so deranged by grief that I had concocted her from thin air?

I left the house. I walked back to the street. (But, again, very slowly.) I got in my car and drove away.

Where she showed up next was the farmers' market.

Of all places, the farmers' market! The one in Waverly. I'd gone there on a Saturday morning to buy salad greens for Nandina. I looked up from the butter lettuce to find Dorothy at the next stall, examining the beets.

She used to act politely bored at farmers' markets. She would accompany me, but just tolerantly, forbearingly, and she would stand around swallowing her yawns while I chose our vegetables for the week.

Also: beets? Beets are so labor-intensive. And they require a certain amount of culinary know-how. Besides which, she didn't much like them. She only agreed to eat them because of the beta-carotene.

But there she stood, lifting a rubber-banded cluster of beets from the heap and studying it seriously, turning it over several times as if trying to *learn* it before setting it back down and picking up another.

I moved toward her as cautiously as if she were some skittish woodland animal. My feet made no sound at all. And when I reached her, I didn't speak. I turned toward the beets myself and selected a bunch of my own. We were standing side by side, so close that even a breath caused our sleeves to whisper together. I could feel the warmth that her skin gave off through the cotton. It warmed my very soul; I can't describe the comfort I felt. I wanted to stand there forever. There was nothing more I could have asked for.

The woman tending the stall said, "Help you?"

I shook my head, almost imperceptibly.

"You'll want to use the tops of these, too," she said. "Notice how fresh and green they are. All you do is boil them up first in a little salted water, say five or so minutes, and then melt you a lump of butter in a . . ."

Hateful woman. Hateful, loud, prattling, cackle-voiced woman. I felt a coolness at my right side, and I knew without looking that Dorothy was gone.

Then she came to Spindle Street.

To the street where my office is.

I'd been to lunch with Peggy and Irene at the little café on the corner. Irene went shoe-shopping afterward, but Peggy and I headed back to work, strolling at a leisurely pace because it happened to be an especially nice day. It was sunny but not too hot, with a little bit of a breeze. And Peggy chose that moment, wouldn't you know, to attempt a heart-to-heart conversation. She must have figured she should seize her chance, since for once we had no audience. She said, "So." And then she said, "Aaron." She said, "So, how has your life been going, Aaron?"

I said, "My life."

"Would you say that you've moved past the very worst of your grief? Or is it still as bad as ever."

"Oh," I said, "well . . ."

"I hope you don't mind my asking."

"No," I said.

Which was true, I found. At that particular moment, I honestly did want to tell somebody what I was feeling. (*Share* with somebody, I very nearly just said—not my usual language at all.)

"In a way," I told Peggy, "it's like the grief has been covered over with some kind of blanket. It's still there, but the sharpest edges are . . . muffled, sort of. Then, every now and then, I lift a corner of the blanket, just to check, and—whoa! Like a knife! I'm not sure that will ever change."

She said, "Is there something the rest of us could be doing to make it easier? Should we talk more about it? Talk less?"

"Oh, no, you've all been—"

Then I sensed a person walking on the curb side of me. She was several feet distant, but she was keeping pace with us. I sensed her roundness, her darkness, her silence, her intense alertness. I didn't dare look over at her, though. I came to a stop. Peggy stopped, too. So did the other person.

I told Peggy, "You go ahead."

"What?"

"Go!"

"Oh!" she said, and one hand flew to the satin bow at her neckline. "Yes, of course!" she said. "I'm so sorry! I'm— Forgive me!"

And she spun away and rushed off.

I would have felt bad about it, except that I couldn't be bothered just then. I waited until she had run up the steps to our building and disappeared inside. Then I turned to Dorothy.

She stood watching me soberly, assessingly. She seemed as real as the NO PARKING sign beside her. Today she wore her black knit top, the one she'd worn the night we first kissed, but it was scrunched beneath the slant of her satchel strap as if she had just come from work.

She said, "I *would* have asked more questions."

"Pardon?"

"We could have talked all along. But you always pushed me away."

"I pushed you away?"

Somebody passed so close that his shoe nicked the tip of my cane, and I turned toward him for one split second, and when I turned back she was gone.

I said, "Dorothy?"

Pedestrians were parting around me like water around a stone, sending me curious glances. Dorothy was nowhere to be seen.

Weeks passed, and all I thought about was how to make her come back.

Was there some theme here? Was there some unifying factor that triggered her visits? The first time, I had been reflecting on our life together; but the second time, I'd been perusing the butter lettuce, for Lord's sake. And the third time, I had been deep in conversation with Peggy. As far as I could determine, each set of circumstances was completely different.

"Nandina," I said one evening, "have you ever . . . Did Mom and Dad ever . . . like, appear to you after they died?"

"Mom and Dad?"

"Or anybody! Grandma Barb, or Aunt Esther . . . You were always close to Aunt Esther, as I recall."

Nandina stopped slicing peaches. (She was making one of her juice drinks for Gil.) She looked at me, and I saw that her eyes were glowing with pity. "Oh, Aaron," she said.

"What."

"Oh, sweetie, I wish there were something I could say."

"What? No, really, I'm fine," I said. "I was just wondering if—"

"I know you must feel as though you're never going to get over this, but, believe me, one day you'll . . . Oh, I don't mean get over it—you'll never really get over it—but one day you're going to wake up and see that you still have your whole life to live."

"I already see that," I said. "What I'm asking—"

"You're only thirty-six! Lots of men haven't even *begun* their lives at thirty-six. You're attractive, and smart. Some really nice woman is going to come along and snap you up one day. You probably can't imagine that, but mark my words. And I want to say right here and now, Aaron, that I would wholeheartedly welcome her. I would welcome anyone you brought home to me, I promise."

"You mean like last time?" I asked.

"You're going to look back and say, 'I can't believe now that I ever thought my life was finished.'"

I could have told her that I worried more about my life stretching on and on. But I didn't want her going all compassionate again.

One late afternoon when I'd stopped by our house, still with no sign of Dorothy, I went around back to where the oak tree used to stand. The tree itself had been carted away at some point, and even the stump had been removed and the hole filled in with wood chips. Gil had arranged for that. I remembered paying the bill, which was considerable.

I was thinking, *Come see this, Dorothy. Come see what changed our world.* But the person who came was old Mimi King, from across the alley. I saw her picking her way through my euonymus bushes. For once she carried no casserole, although she did have a bib apron on. Her gray hair was rolled into little pink curlers that bobbed all over her head. "Why, Aaron!" she said. "How nice to find you at home! I looked out my kitchen window and all at once there you were."

"Hi, Mimi," I said.

She arrived next to me, breathless, and gazed down at where the tree had stood. "If that is not the sorriest sight," she told me.

"Yes, well, it had a good long life, I guess."

"Nasty old thing," she said.

"Mimi," I said, "how long is it since your husband died?"

"Oh, it's been thirty-three years now. Thirty-four. Can you imagine? I've been a widow longer than I've been a wife."

"And did you ever, for instance . . . feel his presence after he died?"

"No," she said, but she didn't seem surprised by the question. "I hoped to, though. I surely hoped to. Sometimes I even spoke out loud to him, in the early years, begging him to show himself. Do you do that with Dr. Rosales?"

"Yes," I said.

I took a deep breath.

I said, "And every now and then, I almost think she *does* show herself."

I sent Mimi a quick sideways glance. I couldn't gauge her reaction.

"I realize that must sound crazy," I said. "But maybe she just hates to see me so sad, is how I explain it. She sees that I can't bear losing her and so she steps in for a moment."

"Well, that's just absurd," Mimi said.

"Oh."

"You think *I* wasn't sad when Dennis died?"

"I didn't mean—"

"You think I could bear losing him? But I had to, didn't I. I had to carry on like always, with three half-grown children depending on me for every little thing. Nobody offered *me* any special consideration."

"Oh, or me, either!" I said.

But she had already turned to go. She flapped one withered arm dismissively behind her as she stalked back toward the alley.

I asked at work. We were sitting around with a birthday cake— Charles's—and paper cups of champagne, and Nandina had just stepped into her office to answer her phone, and I was feeling, I suppose, a little emboldened by the champagne. I said, "Let me just ask you all this. Has anyone here ever felt that a loved one was watching over them?"

Peggy looked up from the candles she was plucking out of the cake, and her eyebrows went all tent-shaped with concern. I had expected that, but I'd figured it was worth a bit of Oh-poor- Aaron, because she was just the kind of person who *would* think her loved ones were watching over her. She didn't speak, though. Irene said, "You mean a loved one who has died?"

"Right."

"This is going to sound weird," Charles said, "but I don't have any loved ones who have died."

"Lucky you," Peggy told him.

"All four of my grandparents passed on long before I was born, and my parents are healthy as horses, knock on wood."

Ho-hum, was all I could think. People who hadn't suffered a loss yet struck me as not quite grown up.

Irene said, "My father died in a car wreck back when I was ten. I remember I used to worry that now he might be all-seeing, and he'd see that I liked to shoplift."

"Ooh, Irene," Charles said. "You shoplifted?"

"I stole lipsticks from Read's Drug Store."

It interested me that Irene imagined the dead might be all-seeing. More than once, since the oak tree fell, I had been visited by the irrational notion that maybe Dorothy knew everything about me now—including some past fantasies having to do with Irene.

"The funny part is," Irene was saying, "back in those days I didn't even *wear* lipstick. And anyhow, I could perfectly well have paid for it. I did get an allowance. I can't explain what came over me."

"But did he find out?" I asked.

"Excuse me?"

"Did your father find out you shoplifted?"

"No, Aaron. How could he do that?"

"Oh. No, of course not," I said.

"Sorry!" Nandina caroled, and out she popped from her office. "That was Hastings Burns, Esquire. Remember Hastings Burns, Esquire? *The Beginner's Legal Reference?*"

"Beginner's Nitpicking," Irene said.

"Beginner's Pain in the Butt," Charles put in.

I was just glad to have the subject switched before Nandina learned what we were talking about.

. . .

Then I was walking toward the post office on Deepdene Road and Dorothy was walking beside me. She didn't "pop up" or anything. She didn't "materialize." She'd just been with me all along, somehow, the way in dreams you'll find yourself with a companion who didn't arrive but is simply there—no explanation given and none needed.

I avoided looking over at her, because I worried I would scare her off. I did slow my pace, though. If anyone had been watching, they'd have thought I was walking a tightrope, I proceeded so carefully.

In front of the post office, I came to a stop. I didn't want to go inside, where there would be other people. I turned to face her. Oh, she looked so . . . Dorothy-like! So normal and clumsy and ordinary, her eyes meeting mine directly, a faint sheen of sweat on her upper lip, her stocky forearms crossing her stomach to hug her satchel close to her body.

I said, "Dorothy, I didn't push you away. How can you say such a thing? Or I certainly didn't mean to. Is that what you think I was doing?"

She said, "Oh, well," and looked off to one side.

"Answer me, Dorothy. Talk to me. Let's talk about this, can't we?"

She drew in a breath to speak, I thought, but then it seemed her attention was snagged by something at her feet. It was her shoe; her left shoe was untied. She squatted and began tying it, hunched over in a mounded shape so I couldn't see her face. I lost patience. "You say *I'm* pushing *you* away?" I asked. "You're the one doing that, damn it!"

She heaved herself up and turned and trudged off, hugging her satchel again. Her orthopedic-looking soles were worn down at the outside edges, and her trouser cuffs were frayed at the bottoms, where she had trod on them. She headed back up Deepdene to Roland Avenue and turned right and I lost sight of her.

You'll wonder why I didn't run after her. I didn't run after her because I was mad at her. Her behavior had been totally unjustified. It had been infuriating.

I kept on standing there long after she had vanished. I no longer had the heart to see to my business at the post office.

Once, we had an author at work who'd written a book of advice for young couples getting married. *Mixed Company*, it was called. He ended up not signing with us—decided we were too expensive and chose an Internet firm instead—but I've never forgotten that title. *Mixed Company*. I'll say. It summed up everything that was wrong with the institution of marriage.

"*Here's* a question," I said to Nate. We were seated at our usual table, waiting for Luke to finish dealing with the salad chef's nervous breakdown. "Have you ever had a visit from anyone who's died?"

"Not a visit in person," Nate said, reaching for the bread basket.

"You've had some other kind of visit?"

"No, but my uncle Daniel—actually my great-uncle—I came across his picture once in the paper."

It seemed to me that Nate might have misunderstood my question, but I didn't interrupt him. He broke open a biscuit. He said, "They had a photo of these government officials in South America. Argentina? Brazil? They'd been arrested for corruption. And there he was, along with a row of other guys. But in full uniform, this time, with a chestload of medals."

"Um . . ."

"It was strange, because I'd definitely seen him in his casket several years before."

"Really," I said.

"You couldn't mistake him, though. Same bent shape to his nose, same hooded look to his eyes. 'So *that's* what you've been up to!' I said."

Then he set his palms on the table and looked around the room. "Any butter in this place?"

I didn't pursue the subject further.

Gil was the only person whose answer made some sense to me.

And I didn't even ask him! I'd have had to be insane—right?—to walk up to my contractor and ask if he'd ever communed with the dead.

All I said was—I was looking at the new bookshelves in the sunporch and I said—"I'm just sorry Dorothy can't see these."

"I'm sorry, too," Gil said. He was squatting to adjust the time on the clock radio on the floor. His men had a habit of plugging it in wherever they were working and just letting the numbers flash 9999 all day, which seemed to irk him.

"She always did want more space for her medical journals," I said.

"Well, these should have made her happy, then," he told me.

He stood up, with a grunt. "Damn. I'm getting old. Did I ever tell you how my dad liked to come back from the dead and check on my work?"

"Uh, no."

"He passed away when I was in high school, but after I went into the building trade I'd catch a glimpse of him from time to time. Just here and there, you know? Kind of shambling around a project, looking to see what was what. He'd grab hold of a corner stud and shake it, testing it out. He'd bend down and pick up a nail that had dropped. Couple of times I got to work in the morning and found this little bunch of nails laid in a row on a sill. God, he did hate waste."

I tried to make out Gil's expression—was he joking?—but he was tipped back on his heels now, squinting up at the frame above one window.

"Must have been a couple of months or so he did that," he went on after a moment. "He never *said* anything. Me, neither. I'd just stand there watching him, wondering what he was after. See, the two of us had not been close. No, sir, not at all. Not since I was a little fellow. He'd disapproved of my riotous manner of living. So I wondered what he was after. Anyhow, he moved on by and by, I can't say exactly when. He just stopped coming around anymore, and eventually I realized. Know what I think now?"

"What," I said.

Gil turned and looked at me. His expression was perfectly serious. "I think I was his unfinished business," he said. "He was sorry he'd given up on me while I was sowing my wild oats, and he came back to make sure I'd turned out okay."

"And so . . . do you figure he accomplished what he wanted?" I asked. "Was he satisfied, in the end?"

"Was he satisfied. Well. Sure, I guess so."

Then he wrote something on the Post-it pad he carried in his shirt pocket, and he tore off the top sheet and slapped it onto the window frame.

I was sitting on a bench in the mall while Nandina was in the Apple Store. I hate malls. I wouldn't have gone with her except her errand was business-related. But the Apple Store was packed, and I started getting restless, so she ordered me out. I sat there all itchy and grumpy and annoyed, but gradually I calmed down. And then I began to understand that Dorothy was sitting next to me.

I didn't speak. I didn't look at her. She didn't speak, either. It seemed we'd agreed to start back at Square One: just *be* together, at first. Just sit. Don't talk; don't ruin things. Just sit there side by side and watch the world go by.

Picture two statues in some Egyptian pyramid: seated man, seated woman, facing forward, receptive.

We watched three old ladies in flowered dresses and huge white spongy jogging shoes, taking their exercise walk. We watched a teenage couple strolling by so entwined and interlaced that you had to wonder how they kept from falling on their faces. We watched a mother scolding a little boy about nine or ten years old. "I just want you to know," she was saying, "that I'm going to have to apologize to your wife every single day of your marriage, for raising such a selfish and inconsiderate person." We sat a long, long time together, absolutely still.

She didn't leave, exactly. It's just that, after a while, I was sitting alone again.

Now that I'd learned to see her, she began showing up more often. It wasn't so much that she arrived as that I would slowly develop an awareness of her presence. She would be the warmth behind me in the checkout line; she'd be the outline on my right as I was crossing the parking lot.

Think of when you're threading your way through a crowd with a friend—how, even if you don't look over, you somehow know your friend is keeping pace with you. That's what it was like with Dorothy. It's the best I can describe it.

Let me say right here and now that I wasn't crazy. Or, to word it a little differently: I was fully aware that seeing a dead person *was* crazy. I didn't honestly believe that the dead came back to earth (came back from where?), and I never, even as a child, thought there were such things as ghosts.

But put yourself in my place. Call to mind a person you've lost that you will miss to the end of your days, and then imagine happening upon that person out in public. You see your long-dead father sauntering ahead with his hands in his pockets. Or you hear your mother behind you calling, "Honey?" Or your little brother who fell through the ice the winter he was six, let's say, passes by with his smell of menthol cough drops and damp mittens. You wouldn't question your sanity, because you couldn't bear to think this wasn't real. And you certainly wouldn't demand explanations, or alert anybody nearby, or reach out to touch this person, not even if you'd been feeling that one touch was worth giving up everything for. You would hold your breath. You would keep as still as possible. You would will your loved one not to go away again.

I discovered that she seemed more comfortable outdoors than indoors. (Which was the opposite of how she had been before she died.) And she stayed away from Nandina's, and she never came to my office. Understandable in both cases, I guess. She and Nandina had always had an edgy relationship, and I think she'd felt like an outsider at my workplace. Not that anyone there had been unfriendly, but you know that office clubbiness, the cozy gossip from desk to desk and the long-standing jokes and the specialized vocabulary.

Harder to figure, though, was that she didn't visit our own house—at least, not the interior. Wouldn't you suppose she'd be interested? The closest she'd come was that time on the sidewalk. But then, one Sunday morning, I caught sight of her in the backyard, beside where the oak tree had been. It was one of the few occasions when she was already in place before I arrived. I glanced out our kitchen window and saw her standing there, looking down at the wood chips, with her hands jammed in the pockets of her doctor coat. I made it to her side in record time, even though I seemed to have left my cane somewhere in the house. I said—slightly short of breath—"You see they removed all the evidence. Ground the stump to bits, even."

"Mmhmm," she said.

"They asked if I wanted to replace it with something, a maple tree or something. Maples are very fast-growing, they said, but I said no. We've never had enough sun here, I said, and maybe now—"

I stopped. This wasn't what I wanted to be talking about. During all the months when she had been absent, there were so many things I had saved up to tell her, so many bits of news about the house and the neighborhood and friends and work and family, but now they seemed inconsequential. Puny. Move far enough away from an event and it sort of levels out, so to speak—settles into the general landscape.

I cleared my throat. I said, "Dorothy."

Silence.

"I can't stand to think that you're dead, Dorothy."

She tore her gaze from the wood chips.

"Dead?" she asked. "Oh, I'm not . . . Well, maybe you *would* call it dead. Isn't that odd."

I waited.

She returned to her study of the wood chips.

"Are you happy?" I asked her. "Do you miss me? Do you miss being alive? Is this hard for you? What are you *going through,* Dorothy?"

She looked at me again. She said, "It's too late to say what I'm going through."

"What? Too late?"

"You should have asked me before."

"Asked you before *what?*" I said. "What are you talking about?"

Then Mimi King called, "Yoo-hoo!" She popped out her back door, waving. She was all dressed up in her church clothes; she even had a hat on. I waved back halfheartedly, hoping this would be enough, but no, on she came, stepping toward us in a wincing manner that meant she must be wearing heels. I said, "Damn," and turned back to Dorothy. But of course she wasn't there anymore.

I knew it was because of Mimi. Why, even while Dorothy was alive she'd had a way of ducking out of a Mimi visit. But somehow I couldn't help taking her disappearance as a reproach to me personally. "You should have asked me before," she'd told me. "It's too late," she'd told me. Then she'd left.

This was all my fault, I couldn't help feeling. Mimi was tripping through my euonymus bushes now, but I turned away with a weight in my chest and limped back into my house.

7

In September, we held a meeting at work to plan for Christmas. Most of us found it difficult to summon up any holiday spirit; temperatures were in the eighties, and the leaves hadn't started turning yet. But we gathered in Nandina's office, Irene and Peggy on the love seat, Charles and I in two desk chairs wheeled in from elsewhere. Predictably, Peggy had brought refreshments—homemade cookies and iced mint tea—which Nandina thanked her for although I knew she didn't see the necessity. ("Sometimes I feel I'm back in grade school," she had told me once, "and Peggy is Class Mother.") I accepted a cookie for politeness' sake, but I let it sit on its napkin on a corner of Nandina's desk.

Irene was wearing her legendary pencil skirt today. It was so narrow that when she was seated she had to hike it above her knees, revealing her long, willowy legs, which she could cross twice over, so to speak, hooking the toe of her upper shoe behind her lower ankle. Peggy was in her usual ruffles, including a sweater with short frilly sleeves because she always claimed Woolcott

Publishing was excessively air-conditioned. And Nandina held court behind her desk in one of her carriage-trade shirtwaists, with her palms pressed precisely together in front of her.

"For starters," she said, "I need to know if any of you have come up with any bright ideas for our holiday marketing."

She looked around the group. There was a silence. Then Charles swallowed a mouthful of cookie and raised his hand a few inches. "This is going to sound a little bit grandiose," he said, "but I think I've found a way to sell people our whole entire *Beginner's* series, all in one huge package."

Nandina looked surprised.

"You've heard of helicopter parents," he told the rest of us. "Those modern-day types who telephone their college kids every hour on the hour just to make sure their little darlings are surviving without them. Nothing *Janie* or I plan to do, believe me—assuming we can ever get the girls to leave home in the first place. But anyhow, this is exactly the kind of gift idea that would appeal to a helicopter parent: we would pack the complete series in a set of handsome walnut-veneer boxes with sliding lids. Open the boxes and you'll find instructions for every conceivable eventuality. Not just the *Beginner's* setting-up-house titles or the *Beginner's* raising-a-family titles but *Beginner's* start-to-finish, cradle-to-grave *living*! And the best part is, the walnut boxes act like modular bookshelf units. Kids would just stack them in their apartments with the tops facing frontwards, slide the lids off, and they're in business. Time to move? They'd slide the lids back on and throw the boxes into the U-Haul. Not ready yet for the breastfeeding book, or the divorce book? Keep those in a box in the basement till they need them."

"What: *Beginner's Retirement,* too?" Irene asked him. "*Beginner's Funeral Planning?*"

"Or toss them into their storage unit," Charles said. "I hear all the kids have storage units now."

Nandina said, "I'm having trouble believing that even helicopter parents would carry things *that* far, Charles."

"Right," Irene said. "Why not just give the parents themselves *The Beginner's Book of Letting Go* and circumvent the whole issue?"

"Do we publish that?" Peggy wondered.

"No, Peggy. I was joking."

"It's a thought, though," Charles said. "But only after we sell the other books, obviously. Make a note of it, Peggy."

"Oh! If we're talking about new titles," Peggy said, perking up, "I have one: *The Beginner's Menopausal Wife.*"

Nandina said, "Excuse me?"

"This man came to fix my stove last week? And he was telling me all about how his wife is driving him crazy going through menopause."

"Honestly, Peggy," Nandina said. "Where do you *find* these people?"

"It wasn't me! My landlord found him."

"You must do something to bring it on, though. Every time we turn around, someone seems to be dumping his life story on you."

"Oh, I don't mind."

"For my own part," Irene said, "I make a practice of keeping things on a purely professional footing. 'Here's the kitchen,' I say, 'here's the stove. Let me know when it's fixed.'"

I laughed, but the others nodded respectfully.

"I promise," Peggy told us, "this was not my fault. The doorbell rang; I answered. This man walked in and said, 'Wife.' Said, 'Menopause.'"

"We seem to be getting away from our subject here," Nandina said. "Does anyone have a suggestion relating to Christmas?"

Charles half raised his hand again. "Well . . ." he said. He looked around at the rest of us. "Not to hog the floor . . ."

"Go ahead," Nandina told him. "You seem to be the only one with any inspiration today."

Charles reached beneath his chair to pick up a book. It was covered in rich brown leather profusely tooled in gold, with Gothic letters spelling out *My Wonderful Life, By.*

"By?" Nandina asked.

"By whomever wants to write it," Charles said.

"*Who*ever," Irene corrected him.

"Oh, I beg your pardon. How gauche of me. See, this would be a gift for the old codger in the family. His children would contract with us to publish the guy's memoirs—pay us up front for the printing, and receive this bound leather dummy with his name filled in. On Christmas morning they'd explain that all he has to do is write his recollections down inside it. After that it goes straight to press, easy-peasey."

He held the book over his head and riffled the pages enticingly.

"What's to stop the codger from just writing stuff on the pages and letting it rest at that?" I asked him.

"All the better for us," Charles said. "Then we've been paid for a printing job we don't have to follow through with. It's strictly non-refundable, you understand."

I refrained from making one of my *Beginner's Flimflam* remarks, but Peggy said, "Oh! His poor children!"

"You pays your money and you takes your chances," Charles told her.

"Maybe we could just offer the dummy by itself—no printing involved," she suggested.

"Then how would that be any different from those *Grandma Remembers* books in the greeting-card stores?"

"It would be more deluxe?"

Charles sighed. "First of all," he said, "people like to see their words printed out. That's what half this company is built upon. And besides that, we're trying to drum up the most expensive product possible."

"But what if his life was *not* wonderful?" Irene asked.

"In that case, he'll be longing to set the record straight. He can hardly wait to get started! He'll be hunched under the Christmas tree already hard at work, scribbling his grievances and ignoring all his relatives."

"Well, thank you, Charles," Nandina said. "That does give us something to think about. The modular-bookshelf idea seems a bit . . . ambitious, but we should definitely consider the memoir plan. Now, anyone else?"

The rest of us took to studying the décor, like students hoping not to be called upon.

One odd effect of Dorothy's visits was that, more and more, I'd begun seeing the world through her eyes. I sat through that meeting like a foreigner, marveling that these people could take such subjects so seriously. Just think: A set of instruction manuals whose stated goal was to skim the surface. A hodgepodge of war recollections and crackpot personal philosophies that no standard publishing house would have glanced at. This was the purpose of my existence?

I used to toy with the notion that when we die we find out what our lives have amounted to, finally. I'd never imagined that we could find that out when somebody else dies.

It was lunchtime when the meeting ended, but instead of going to the corner café with the others I retreated to my office. I had some work to catch up on, I told them. Once I was alone, though, I swiveled my desk chair toward the window and stared out blankly at the dingy brick landscape. It was a relief to stop looking animated, to drop my expression of lively engagement.

I thought back to the time when Dorothy had stood on Rumor Road gazing at our house. I thought of when she'd walked alongside me after lunch. It occurred to me that, in all probability, neither one of us had actually spoken aloud during our encounters. Our conversations had played out silently in my head—my words flowing smoothly, for once, without a single halt or stutter. Granted, that was how I tended to recall *all* my conversations. I might ask somebody, "C-c-could you give—give—address," but in my mind it was an unhesitating "Could you give me your address, please?" Still, I never fooled myself. I knew how I really sounded. I sounded like a breaking-up cell-phone call.

With Dorothy's visits, though, it had been different. I had glided through my sentences effortlessly, because I had spoken just in my thoughts. And she had understood my thoughts. It had all been so easy.

Except now I wanted the jolts and jogs of ordinary life. I wanted my consonants interrupting my vowels as I spoke, my feet stubbing hers as we hugged, my nose bumping hers as we kissed. I wanted *realness,* even if it was flawed and pockmarked.

I closed my eyes, and I willed her with all my heart just to come lay a hand on my shoulder. But she didn't.

I heard the others returning from lunch—scraps of chatter and laughter. A chair scraped. A telephone rang. Several minutes later, someone tapped on my door.

I swiveled to face forward. "Who is it?" I said. ("Who?" is what I really said.)

The door opened a few inches and Peggy poked her head in. "Are you busy?" she asked.

"Well . . ."

She stepped inside and shut the door carefully behind her. (Oh-oh: another of her heart-to-hearts.) She was holding one hand out, palm up, displaying a cookie on a napkin. "You left this on Nandina's desk," she told me, and she placed it on my blotter. "I thought you might want it, since you didn't go to lunch."

"Thanks."

Under her arm she carried her cookie tin, which was painted with pink and lavender hydrangeas. The edge of a paper lace doily peeked out from under the lid. She placed the tin on my blotter, too, but she made no mention of it, as if she were hoping to sneak it past me.

"It was Reuben day at the Gobble-Up," she said. "We all ordered grilled Reubens."

"Great. I'll be the only one fit to work this afternoon."

"Yes, I've already got a tummy ache."

I waited for her to leave, but instead she pulled up the chair across from my desk. She perched on only the front few inches of it, though. I considered that a good sign. But then she removed her sweater, which was definitely a bad sign. She turned to drape it just so over the back of the chair, prinking out the short sleeves so that they flared like hollyhocks. Then she faced me again. She clasped her hands in her lap. "I guess they didn't think too much of my idea," she said.

"What idea was that?"

"My menopausal-wife idea. Don't you even remember it?"

"Oh, yes," I said.

I tried to cast my mind back to the menopausal wife.

"Well," I said after a pause, "maybe since we were focused on Christmas . . ."

"No, it's always like that. Nandina's always telling me, 'You're a full player on the team, Peggy; I don't know where we'd be without you, Peggy,' but then, when I speak up, I always get shot down. They didn't spend one second's thought on what I said this morning, except to laugh at me for having a conversation with my repairman. They didn't discuss it, didn't vote on it; then Nandina ups and tells Charles that he's the only one with any inspiration. Did you not notice how she said that? But it was a *good* idea! They should have paid it more attention!"

"Well, I wonder . . ." I said. I was still trying to recollect what her idea had consisted of, exactly. "I wonder if maybe people thought it was a little too . . . specialized."

"Specialized! Half the world's population goes through menopause. It's not what you would call a rare and exotic condition."

"Yes, all right, but . . . Or maybe it's just that the focus seems odd. *Beginner's Menopause* I can see, but *Beginner's Menopausal Wife*? That seems aimed at the wrong reader."

"It is *not* aimed at the wrong reader," Peggy said. She was sitting extremely straight-backed now, and her clasped hands were white at the fingertips. "It's aimed at exactly the person who should have this information: the husband. He's bewildered! He's saying, 'What's going on with this woman? I don't understand!' And we would be explaining to him what she is experiencing. We'd tell him what she needs from him, how she's feeling useless and outdated now, and how he should be taking extra care of her."

Yes, that *would* be Peggy's main thrust. I said, "Look, Peggy. I see your point, but some people hate being fussed over; have you considered that? If his wife is feeling useless, maybe she'd feel even more useless if her husband started babying her. Maybe she'd even resent it."

"That is so, so like you," Peggy said.

"What?"

"Only you would think of *resenting* someone's doing you a kindness."

"I just meant—"

"*Normal* people say, 'Why, thank you, dear. This makes me feel much better, dear. It makes me feel loved and valued.'"

"Okay . . ."

"But *you:* oh, no. You act so sensitive, so prickly; we all just walk on eggshells around you in case we might say the wrong thing."

I said, "How did we end up with *me,* all of a sudden?"

"It's not fair, Aaron. You expect too much of us. We're not mind-readers! We're all just doing our best here; we don't know;

we're just trying to get through life as best we can, like everybody else!"

Then she jumped up and tore out of the room, slamming the door behind her.

Goodness.

I was left gaping, completely at a loss. I had seldom been involved in a conversation so illogical. Point A had led not to Point B but to Point H. Points X, Y, Z, even!

I needed a book called *The Beginner's Demented Secretary.*

Had the others overheard? They couldn't have missed that epic door slam, at least. I listened for voices, but I didn't hear any. In fact, it was way too quiet.

I picked up the cookie on my blotter and studied it. I felt sort of unsettled. I'd never seen Peggy lose her temper before.

The cookie was oatmeal-chocolate chip. It wasn't a flat disk, like the kind you buy in stores; it was a big, humped hillock of a thing, lumpy with whole oats and studded with extra-large bits of chocolate, not chips so much as chunks. I took an experimental nibble. The chocolate lay coolly on my tongue a few seconds before it melted. The dough had been baked exactly the right length of time—some might say underbaked, but not I—and it was chewy inside but crisp outside, with some tiny sharp pieces of something that provided a textural contrast. Nuts, maybe? No, not nuts. Harder than nuts; more edgy than nuts. I really didn't know. I seemed to have finished the cookie while I was deliberating, so I pried the lid off the tin and selected another. I needed to pin this thing down. I bit off a mouthful and chewed thoughtfully. The oats had their own distinct identity; I suspected they were the old-fashioned kind, rather than the quick-cooking. I would have liked a glass of cold milk but you can't have everything. I finished that cookie and reached for another. Then another. I feel sort of silly saying this, but as I chewed I closed my eyes, in order to savor the different textures and to feel the oases of chocolate melting on my tongue. Then I swallowed and opened my eyes and took another bite.

Peggy's cookie tin sat on my desk, another thing to savor, somehow nourishing to my vision. For each season, she had an appropriate tin: a shiny red one at Christmas with a Santa Claus on the lid, a pale-green one at Easter featuring a rabbit in a bonnet, and these hydrangeas till fall arrived, when out came her acorn tin. I started on a new cookie. Chewing steadily, I transferred my gaze to the sweater she'd left hanging on the back of the chair. It wasn't clear to me how a short-sleeved sweater could provide much warmth, but she seemed very fond of this one, which was white and sort of gathered at the shoulders, so that it swung out like a cape. The sleeves were hemmed with narrow knit ruffles (wouldn't you know), and two more ruffles ran down the straight part where the buttons were. Why, I would bet that even Peggy's underwear was ruffled. I spent a pleasurable moment picturing that: a bra trimmed with eyelet lace like the cookie tin's paper doily, stretched flat where it bridged the soft dip between her breasts. I reached inside the tin for another cookie, but it seemed I'd finished them. All I found were crumbs. I pressed a fingertip to the crumbs and licked them off, every last one of them. Then I gave a long, contented sigh and leaned back in my chair and swiveled toward the window again.

This was a rear window, ground-floor level, and filmed with dust, facing the back of a shabby brick building hung with peeling wooden porches. Beneath the porches was a row of trash cans and empty milk crates, and in front of those, so motionless that it took me a second to realize, stood Dorothy.

She was some twenty feet distant from me, on the far side of the alley, and I couldn't tell if she saw me. She was looking toward my window, though. Her arms hung empty at her sides, and she wasn't wearing her satchel. This gave her the air of someone who didn't know what to do with herself. She seemed lost, almost. She seemed uncertain where to go next.

I scrambled to my feet, but before I could get the window open she turned and wandered away.

8

One night I woke up and heard low murmurs from Nandina's bedroom. And one morning a few days later, when I was shaving in the bathroom, I chanced to look out the window and see Gil Bryan walking from the house toward the street, climbing into his pickup and starting it and quietly rolling away.

Oh, I was cramping their style, all right. It was time I moved back home.

Work was still going on there, as both Nandina and Gil pointed out when I mentioned my plans that evening. But really I could have returned several weeks ago, if I didn't mind having the men overlap me a bit in the mornings. When I said as much to Nandina and Gil, they said, "Oh. Well . . . ," and, "If you're sure, then . . . ," and both of them looked relieved. I started packing right after supper. I moved the next afternoon, a Friday, taking off early from the office.

The main part of my house was bare and shiny and echoing, as pristine as an empty dollhouse. But stray furniture and packed cartons filled every inch of my bedroom, so I settled in the guest room, which was small enough to have escaped being used for storage. I was glad to have an excuse not to return to my own bed. I think I was afraid it would bring back too many memories—not from the days of my marriage but from those weeks after the oak tree fell, when I'd lain there alone night after night wondering how to go on.

It wasn't only for Gil and Nandina's sake that I moved back when I did. Let's be honest. The other reason, the main reason, was that I was hoping I would see Dorothy there. In the two weeks since her appearance outside my office window, there had been no sign of her, not a glimmer. I had looked for her in vain on the sidewalks and in crowds and wherever anonymous strangers waited in line. I had spun around without warning as I stood at intersections, hoping to surprise her behind me. I had settled conspicuously on public benches and strained to feel her sleeve brushing my sleeve. Nothing. She was avoiding me.

At home, I focused on the places where she had shown up before: the street and the backyard. On Saturday I got up when it was barely light out, and after a makeshift breakfast—two granola bars from a carton of foodstuffs in the bedroom—I took a stroll around the block, pegging my cane against the sidewalk almost soundlessly so as not to wake the neighbors. All I saw was one black cat, an insultingly paranoid type who shrank off as I drew near. The solitude made me feel too tall. I was glad to get back to the house.

Once the sun was fully up, I dragged a wrought-iron chair from the front yard to the rear. I set it on the back stoop and sat down, facing outward. My God, the lawn was a wreck. We'd had a dry summer, and the grass was more like straw. The azaleas looked stunted and wizened, and the wood-chip circle where the oak tree once stood had sunk in a good foot or more.

I was probably out of my mind to imagine that Dorothy would come here. The backyard was so bald. It lacked camouflage. There weren't enough dapplings of shadow to break up the flat glare of the sun.

I rose, eventually, and went into the house for my keys and drove to the grocery store, where I gathered a large amount of provisions. You'd have thought I was shopping for a family of ten. (I think I had it in mind to *hole up,* to wait it out in my cave until Dorothy chose to show herself, however long it might take.) Back home I dug a few kitchen utensils out of the bedroom cartons and I fixed myself a conscientiously balanced lunch—protein, starch, green vegetable—after which I went out and sat in the wrought-iron chair again, for lack of anything better to do. A few minutes of this and I rose to uncoil the garden hose. The grass made a bristly sound under my feet. I placed the sprinkler near the azaleas and turned the faucet on full-blast and sat back down. And that was how I discovered the pleasures of watching a lawn being watered.

I swear that I could feel the grass's gratitude. The birds seemed grateful, too. A little crowd of them came out of nowhere, as if word had gotten around somehow, and they twittered and chirped and fluttered in the droplets. My chair was too right-angled, forcing me to sit unnaturally erect, and its scrolls and curlicues dug into the knobs of my spine, but even so I felt the most pervasive sense of peace. I tilted my face up and squinted against the sunlight to follow the arc of the spray, which sashayed left, sashayed right, like a young girl swishing her skirts as she walked.

I practically drowned that yard.

Not till early evening, when the gnats started biting, did I turn off the hose. Then I went inside to fix dinner, and after that I tried to read a while in the impractical little slipper chair in one corner of the guest room. But I was so unaccountably, irresistibly sleepy that I laid aside my book fairly soon and went to bed. I slept without so much as a twitch, I believe, until nearly nine the next morning.

The early part of Sunday I spent dragging various cartons from the bedroom to the kitchen, replacing pots and dishes and foods in the cabinets that smelled of fresh paint. I enjoyed establishing just the right locations for things. I never could have done that in the old days—at least not with any hope that they would stay there, not with Dorothy around.

When I caught myself thinking this, I averted my head sharply, as if I could shake the thought away.

Once I'd unpacked what I could, I went out back again, like some kind of sports fan desperate to return to his game. The grass was still a yellowish white, although it no longer crunched. I moved the sprinkler over by the euonymus alongside the alley, sinking into the sodden earth with every step, and I turned the water on and settled back into my chair.

I had learned by now that when the sunlight hit the spray in a certain way I could occasionally, almost, see things. I mean things that weren't really there. Not Dorothy, unfortunately. But one time I saw this sort of column, an ornate Corinthian column rising up and sprouting apart at the top and then dissolving into particles, and another time a woman in a long beige dress with a bustle. And yet another time—this was the weirdest—I saw an entire swing set, and a man in shirtsleeves was pushing a small child in one of those chair-like swings intended for infants and toddlers. I also saw a good many rainbows, needless to say, and numerous sheets of changeable taffeta unfurling and spreading themselves across the lawn.

But never Dorothy.

I saw a woman with an umbrella but—hey!—she was real. She was Mimi King, hovering by the euonymus bushes and shifting from foot to foot like a girl preparing to enter the arc of a jump rope, until finally she plunged into the spray and emerged on the other side of it, shaking out her umbrella before she collapsed it. "Well, hi there, Aaron!" she called, and she squished toward me in her Sunday heels, no doubt digging little tent-peg holes as she came. When she reached me, I stood up and said, "Good morning, Mimi."

"At this rate," she said, "you'll be growing yourself a rain forest!"

"Got to do my bit for the planet," I told her.

She placed the tip of her umbrella between her feet and rested both hands on the handle. "Have you moved back in?" she asked.

"I figured it was time."

"We were all afraid you might be gone for good."

"*Oh,* no," I said, as if I hadn't had the same thought myself once.

"I was asking Mary-Clyde just last week; I said, 'Shouldn't somebody let him know that that lawn service of his is mowing grass that's not even there anymore?' But Mary-Clyde said, 'Oh, I'm sure he must be aware; he's got those construction men around; I'm sure they would have told him.' 'Well, I don't know about that,' I said. 'I don't feel construction men are very *sensitive* to lawns.'"

"Would you care to sit down, Mimi?" I asked. I felt bad about her shoes, which were plastered with a good half-inch of mud and damp yellow grass blades.

But she was pursuing her own line of thought. "This is just providential," she said, "because I've been thinking I would like to have you over for dinner some night."

"Oh, well, I'm not—I'm not—"

"I would like for you to meet my niece. She's had a hard time of it since she lost her husband, and I'm thinking it would do her good to talk to you."

"I'm not all that social," I told her.

"Of course you're not! Don't you think I realize that? But this is different. Louise lost her husband last Christmas Eve morning, can you imagine? Poor thing has been just devastated."

"Christmas Eve?" I said. "Haven't I heard about this person?"

"Oh, well, you *know,* then! She'd accepted that he had a terminal illness, but it never entered her mind that he would pass on Christmas Eve."

"Yes," I said, "I guess she won't celebrate Christmas ever again without remembering that."

I was just trying to sound sympathetic, but it seemed I'd succeeded too well, because Mimi gave me a look of surprise and said, "That's exactly right! See? You would have so much to say to her!"

"No, no!" I hurried to say. "No, believe me, it's not as if I could offer her any . . . household hints or anything."

"Household hints?"

"Besides, for the next little bit I'm going to be busy setting things straight. My golly, the place is a mess! I've got everything stuffed in one room: furniture, books, bric-a-brac, lamps, curtains, rugs. . . ."

I drove her away with words, finally. She gave me a wilted little wave and started back toward the alley, raising her umbrella again as she approached the sprinkler, although I'd gallantly shut the faucet off the instant she turned to leave. Anyhow, I had to admit the lawn was pretty well watered by now.

Having reminded myself of the mess in the bedroom, I went to tackle it after lunch. There wasn't much point in putting things back in place yet, since they would only hamper the workmen, but I figured I could probably discard some stuff ahead of time. Dorothy's medical books, for instance, and maybe a few of those decorative doodads that tended to accumulate for no useful purpose.

It turned out that a good many of the books had gotten damp—not just Dorothy's but mine as well. They had dried in the months since, more or less, but their covers had buckled and they had a moldy, mousy smell. Carton after carton I would open, dig through dispiritedly, and then drag to the front hall for Gil's men to carry out to the alley. I did try to save a few of my favorite biographies, though, and the family photo albums. I'd appropriated the albums after our mother died, and I felt guilty about the state they were in. I took them to the kitchen and spread them across the table and all available counters, where I pried the faded black pages apart in hopes that they would air out.

With the doodads, I was more callous. What did I care about my bronzed baby shoes? (A pair of tiny Nikes; how witty.) Or the little china clock that always ran slow, or the tulip-shaped vase someone had given us when we got married?

I ate supper standing up, since the table was covered with albums. I cruised around the kitchen studying sepia-colored photos as I munched on my taco. Men in high collars, women in leg-of-mutton sleeves, solemn-faced children whose clothes looked stiff as sandwich boards. Nobody was identified. I guess the album-keeper had thought they didn't *need* to be identified; everybody knew who everybody was in those days, in that smaller world. But then the sepia changed to black-and-white, and then to garish Kodacolor, and none of those photos bore any labels, either—not my parents getting married, or Nandina in her christening gown, or the two of us attending a children's birthday party. Nor did the single snapshot from my own wedding: Dorothy and I standing side by side on the front steps of my parents' church, looking uncomfortable and uncertain. We were both of us badly dressed—I in a brown suit that left my wrist bones exposed, Dorothy in a bright-blue knit stretched too tightly across the mound of her stomach. Fifty years from now, strangers discovering this album at some parking-lot flea market would glance at us and flip the page, not even interested enough to wonder who we'd been.

Gil's men and I barely crossed paths, since we had such different schedules. They arrived each weekday morning just as I was finishing breakfast. They brought paper cups of coffee that steamed in the early coolness, and they scuffed their soles heavily on the hall mat to let me know they were here. After we'd exchanged a few weather remarks I would leave for work, and by the time I returned they were already gone, no sign of them remaining but their little nest of belongings on a scrunched-up drop cloth in one corner of the living room. Something hung on in the atmosphere, though—something more than the scent of their cigarette smoke. I felt I'd interrupted a conversation about richer, fuller lives than mine, and when I drifted through the bare rooms it wasn't only to reclaim my house; it was also, just a little bit, in the hope that some of that richness might have been left behind for me.

On Friday, however, two of the men were still there when I got home. One was just completing the varnishing of the sunporch floor while the other walked around collecting paint cans, brushes, and rollers in an empty cardboard carton. "We were figuring we'd be gone by now," the one with the carton told me, "but then Gary here bought the wrong color varnish and set us back some."

"It wasn't my fault, bro!" Gary said. "It was Gil the one wrote the wrong number down."

"Whatever," the other man said. "Anyways, we're finished," he told me. "Hope you like how it all turned out."

"You mean you're *finished* finished?" I asked.

"Yup."

"Nothing more needs doing?"

"Not unless you say so."

I looked around me. The place was spotless—the living-room walls a gleaming white, the new bookshelves in the sunporch just waiting to be filled. Somebody had swept up the last traces of sawdust, and the paper cups and the jar-lid ashtrays had disappeared, which made me feel oddly forlorn.

"No," I said, "I can't think of a thing."

Gary straightened and laid his brush across the top of his can. "Now, don't go walking on this, you hear?" he said. "Not for twenty-four hours. And then, the next few days or so, keep your shoes on. You wouldn't believe how many folks think they're doing a floor a favor to take their shoes off and walk in their stocking feet. But that's the *worst* thing."

"Worst thing in the world," the other man agreed.

"Heat of your body . . ." Gary said.

"Linty old socks . . ."

"Bottoms of your feet mashing flat against the wood . . ."

They were still moaning and shaking their heads when Gil opened the front door. I knew it was Gil because he always knocked before he let himself in. "Hey there, guys," he said, appearing in the living-room archway. He wore his after-hours outfit: khakis and a clean shirt. "Hey, Aaron."

"Hi, Gil."

"How we coming along?"

"Just finishing up, boss," the man with the carton said.

Gil walked over to inspect the sunporch floor. "Looks good," he said. "Now, give it twenty-four hours before you step on it," he told me, "and then for a few days after that—"

"I know: not in my stocking feet," I said.

"Worst thing in the world," he said.

He saw the men out to the hall, then, clapping Gary on the shoulder, reminding them both they were due at Mrs. McCoy's early Monday morning. (I felt a little twinge of sibling rivalry.) Then he returned to the living room.

"So," I said, "I hear you're all done here."

My voice echoed hollowly in the empty room.

"She's good as new," Gil told me.

"Actually, better than new," I said. "I appreciate the care you took, Gil."

"Oh, any time. God forbid."

"God forbid," I agreed.

"Monday I'll send a couple of men to move the furniture back. You want to be here for that?"

"No, that's okay. It's pretty cut-and-dried, in a house this small."

He nodded. He pivoted to survey the living room. "And window washers," he said. "You'll be needing those. We've got a list of names, if you want."

"I'm sure Nandina knows someone."

"Oh," Gil said suddenly.

He clapped a hand to the right front pocket of his khakis. A certain staginess in the gesture caught my attention. "By the way," he said, falsely casual. He pulled a tiny blue velvet box from his pocket, clearly a ring box.

"Oho!" I said.

"Yeah, well . . ."

He snapped the lid open and stepped closer to show me. (I caught a strong scent of aftershave.) The ring was yellow gold, set with a little winking diamond.

"That's really pretty, Gil," I said. "Who's it for?"

"Ha ha ha."

"Does she know about this?"

"Just in theory. We've had the talk about getting married. Gee," he said, "I guess I should have asked you first. I mean asked for her hand or something."

"Take it," I said, and I gave him a breezy wave.

"Thanks," he said with a grin. He looked down at the ring. "I know the stone is kind of small, but the jeweler claimed it's flawless. Not the least little flaw, he said. I had to take his word for it. Would I know a flaw if I saw one?"

"She's going to love it," I told him.

"I hope so." He was still studying it.

"How did you know what size to buy?"

"I traced the band of that opal of hers when she was in the shower once."

He reddened and glanced up at me, maybe worrying he had revealed more than he should have, and I said, "Well, great. I can't think of anyone I'd rather have for a brother-in-law."

"Thanks, Aaron." He closed the box and returned it to his pocket. "There's a wedding ring that matches it, but I figured I should make sure Nandina likes this before I buy it. I already know she wants *me* to wear a ring."

"Yes, that's how people do these days," I said. I started to raise my left hand to show him my own ring, which I still wore, but then I thought—I don't know. It seemed that might have been tactless, somehow.

No couple buying wedding rings wants to be reminded that someday one of them will have to accept the other one's ring from a nurse or an undertaker.

It was kind of a nuisance having to wait till Monday for the furniture moving. I started doing some of the work ahead of time—dragging the living-room rug into place and unrolling it, setting a few of the lighter-weight objects where they belonged. And on Saturday evening, when the sunporch floor was dry, I fitted what books I still owned into the new bookshelves. I carried the photo albums from the kitchen and lined them up in order, oldest first. Even the most recent wasn't all *that* recent. The last picture in that album—my mother's butterfly bush in full bloom—came immediately after our wedding photo, so I'm guessing it dated from late summer of 1996. Or '97 at the latest, because my father died in early '98, and he was the one who took the pictures in our family.

This business of not labeling photos reminded me of those antique cemeteries where the names have worn off the gravestones and you can't tell who is buried there. You see a little gray tablet with a melted-looking lamb on top, and you know it must have been somebody's child who died, but now you can't even make out her name or the words her parents chose to say how much they missed her. It's just so many random dents in the stone, and the parents are long gone themselves, and everything's been forgotten.

Even my mother's butterfly bush struck me as poignant, with its show-offy clusters of blossoms in a vibrant, electric purple. Although in fact that bush still existed; it stood right there in Nandina's backyard, where I could see it every time I took the garbage out.

In our wedding photo Dorothy did not, of course, carry her satchel, but her dress-up purse was almost equally bulky and utilitarian—a heavy brown leather rectangle with a strap that crossed her chest in the same theft-deterrent fashion. She had said, "Would you like me to wear a white gown? I could do that. I wouldn't mind. I could ask if our receptionist would take me to this place she knows. I thought maybe something, oh, not strapless or anything but maybe with a scoop neck, white but not shiny, not lacy, just a *lustrous* white, you know what I mean? And I was thinking a bouquet of all white flowers. Baby's breath and white roses and . . . are orange blossoms white? I do know they're not orange, although it sounds as if they would be. I'm not talking about a veil or anything. I'm not talking about a long train or anything like that. But something elegant and classic, to mark the occasion. You think?"

"Oh, God, no. Good Lord, no," I said.

"Oh."

"We're neither one of us the type for that, thank heaven," I said.

"No, of course not," she said.

In the photograph her blue knit was not very becoming, but in real life it had looked fine, as far as I can recall. (Photos have a way of *frumping* people; have you noticed?) Anyhow, I had never paid much heed to such things. At the time I was just glad that I'd landed the woman I wanted. And I believe that she was glad to have landed me—the diametrical opposite of that needy "roommate" who had demanded too much of her.

Then why was our marriage so unhappy?

Because it *was* unhappy. I will say that now. Or it was difficult, at least. Out of sync. Uncoordinated. It seemed we just never quite got the hang of being a couple the way other people did. We should have taken lessons or something; that's what I tell myself.

Once, when we had an anniversary coming up—our fifth, I believe—I invited her out to dinner. "I was thinking of the Old Bay," I told her. "The first place I ever took you to."

"The Old Bay," she said. "Really. Are you forgetting that we couldn't even see to read the menus there?"

"Oh, okay," I said, but I felt a little disappointed. For sentiment's sake, at least, you would think she could have agreed to it. "Where, then?" I asked.

"Maybe Jean-Christophe?"

"Jean-Christophe! Good grief!"

"What's wrong with that?"

"Jean-Christophe is so pretentious. They bring you these teeny froufrou bites to eat between courses, and you have to make a big show of being surprised and thankful."

"So *don't* make a show," she said. "Just fold your arms across your chest and glower."

"Very funny," I told her. "What on earth made you think of Jean-Christophe? Is this another one of your receptionist's ideas? Jean-Christophe didn't even exist, back when you and I were courting."

"Oh, I didn't realize it had to have historical significance."

"Dorothy," I said. "Would you rather just not do this?"

"I said I would, didn't I? But then all you can come up with is this fusty old place where your parents used to eat. And when I question it, you fly into a huff and turn down everything else I suggest."

"I didn't turn down 'everything else'; I turned down Jean-Christophe. It just so happens that I dislike a restaurant where the waiters require more attention than my date does."

"Where *would* you be willing to eat, then?"

"Oh, shoot," I said, "I don't care. Let's just go to Jean-Christophe."

"Well, if you don't care, why do we bother?"

"Are you deliberately trying to misunderstand me?" I asked her. "I care that we have a good meal together, preferably without feeling like we're acting in some kind of play. And I was thinking it might be a place with associations for the two of us. But if you're so set on Jean-Christophe, fine; we'll go to Jean-Christophe."

"Jean-Christophe was just a suggestion. There are lots of other possibilities."

"Like where?"

"Well, how about Bo Brooks?"

"Bo Brooks! A crab house? For our anniversary?"

"We did go to Bo Brooks a couple of times while we were dating. It would certainly meet the 'associations' criterion."

"Yes, but—"

I stopped and looked at her.

"You really don't get it, do you," I said.

"What don't I get?"

"Never mind."

"I'm not *ever* going to get it if you refuse to discuss it," she said, and now she was using her doctor voice, her super-calm, let's-be-reasonable voice. "Why don't you just begin at the beginning, Aaron, and tell me exactly what you envision for our anniversary dinner."

"How about what *you* envision?" I said. "Can't you be bothered coming up with any ideas of your own?"

"I already offered an idea of my own. I offered two ideas, as I recall, and you rejected both of them. So it's back in your court now, Aaron."

Why am I telling this story?

I forget.

And I forget where we ended up eating, too. Someplace or other; I don't remember. What I do remember is that familiar, weary, helpless feeling, the feeling that we were confined in some kind of rodent cage, wrestling together doggedly, neither one of us ever winning.

I was rinsing vegetables for my supper, and I turned from the sink to reach for a towel, and I saw Dorothy.

"You're here," I said.

She was standing next to me, so close that she'd had to step back a bit to give me room when I turned. She wore one of her plain white shirts and her usual black pants, and her expression was grave and considering—her head cocked to one side and her eyebrows raised.

"I thought you might never come again," I said.

She appeared unsurprised by this, merely nodding and continuing to study me, so that it seemed I'd been right to worry.

"Was it the cookies?" I asked. "Were you upset that I ate Peggy's cookies?"

"You should have told me you liked cookies," she said, and I don't know why I'd ever doubted that she actually spoke on these visits, because her voice was absolutely real—low and somewhat flat, very level in tone.

I said, "What? I don't like cookies!"

"I could have baked you cookies," she said.

"What are you talking about? Why would I want you to bake cookies? How come we're wasting this time discussing *cookies*, for God's sake?"

"You're the one who brought them up," she said.

Had I lived through this whole scene before? I felt tired to death all of a sudden.

She said, "I used to think it was your mother's fault. She was such a fusser; no wonder you fended people off the way you did. But then I thought, *Oh, well: fault.* Who's to say why we let one person influence us more than another? Why not your father? *He* didn't fuss."

"I fended people off?" I said. "That's not fair, Dorothy. How about how *you* behaved? Wearing your white coat even to go out to dinner; carrying your big satchel. 'I'm Dr. Rosales,' you'd say. Always so busy, so businesslike. Bake cookies? You never even made me a cup of tea when I had a cold!"

"And if I had? What would you have done?" she asked. "Swatted the cup away, I guarantee it. Oh, it used to bother me when I saw what people thought of me. Your mother and your sister, the people in your office . . . I'd see your secretary thinking, *Poor, poor Aaron, his wife is so coldhearted. So unnurturing, so ungiving. Doesn't value him half as much as the rest of us do.* 'Shows what *you* know,' I wanted to tell her. 'Why didn't he marry someone else if he was so keen on nurturing? If I'd behaved any other way, do you suppose he and I would ever have gotten together?'"

I said, "That wasn't why we got together."

"Oh, wasn't it?" she said.

She turned away to gaze out the window over the sink. Earlier I'd switched the sprinkler back on, and I could see how her eyes followed the to-and-fro motion. "I had a job offer in Chicago," she told me in a reflective tone. "You never knew that. This was one of my old professors, somebody I looked up to. He offered me a much better job than what I had here—not better paying, maybe, but more prestigious and more interesting. I felt honored that he even remembered me. But you and I had just gone to our first movie together, and I couldn't think of anything but you."

I stared at her. I felt as if heavy furniture were being moved around in my head.

"Even after we were married," she said, "I'd have patients now and then who wore braces or splints or the like with Velcro fasteners, and they'd be undressing in a treatment room, and from my office I'd hear that ripping sound as the fasteners came apart, and I would think, *Oh!* I would think of you."

I wanted to step closer to her but I was afraid I would scare her off. And she didn't seem encouraging. She kept her face set toward the window, her eyes fixed on the sprinkler.

I said, "I probably did save up that barberry thorn."

I wasn't sure she would understand what I was referring to, so I added, "Not to make you feel bad about the L.A. trip, though. Just, maybe, subconsciously to . . . oh, let you know I needed you, maybe."

Now she did look at me.

"We should have gone to Bo Brooks," I said. "Who cares if it's a crab house? We would have gotten all dressed up, you in the beautiful long white gown you were married in and me in my tuxedo, and we'd eat out on the deck, where everybody else was wearing tank tops and jeans. When we walked past they would stare at us, and we'd give them gracious little Queen Elizabeth waves, and they would laugh and clap. Your train would be a bit of a problem—it would catch on the splintery planking—so I'd scoop it up in my arms and carry it behind you to our table. 'Two dozen of your jumbos and a pitcher of cold beer,' I'd tell the waitress once we were seated, and she'd roll out the big sheets of brown paper, and then here would come the crabs, steaming hot, dumped between us in this huge orange peppery heap."

Dorothy still didn't speak, but I could see that her expression was softening. She might even have been starting to smile, a little.

"The waitress would ask if we wanted bibs but we would say no, that was for tourists. And then we'd pick up our mallets and we'd be sitting there banging away like kindergarteners at Activity Hour, with bits of shell flying up and sticking to your dress and my tux, but we would just laugh; what would we care? We would just laugh and go on hammering."

Dorothy was smiling for real now, and her face seemed to be shining. In fact she was shining all over, and growing shimmery and transparent. It was sort of like what you see when you swerve your eyes as far to the left as you can without turning your head, so you can glimpse your own profile. First your profile is there and then it's half not there; it's nothing but a thread of an outline. And then she was gone altogether.

9

I never saw Dorothy again after that. I did keep an eye out, at first, but underneath I think I knew that she had left for good.

Nowadays, I step into the backyard without the slightest expectation that I'll meet her. I hoist Maeve into her toddler seat and start her gently swinging, and all I have on my mind is what a beautiful Saturday morning it is. Even this early in the day, the sunshine feels like melting liquid on my skin.

"More, Daddy! More!" Maeve says. "More" is her favorite word, which tells you a lot about her. More hugs, more songs, more tickle-game, more of the world in general. She's one of those children who seem overjoyed to find themselves on this planet—a sturdy little blond squiggle-head with a preference for denim overalls and high-top sneakers, the better for climbing, running, rolling down hills, getting into trouble.

I have become expert at grabbing the back of the swing seat in the very center, so that, even one-handed, I can send it off perfectly straight. When it returns I push it higher by pressing a palm against the puff of denim ballooning between the slats. (Underneath her overalls, Maeve still wears diapers. Although we're working on that.) She bends double over the front bar and wriggles her legs ecstatically, skewing her trajectory, but I'm patient; when the swing approaches again, I grab the top slat to restart her. We have a couple of hours to fill before her mother gets home from her errands.

"Here goes," I say, and Maeve says, "Whee!" I don't know where she learned that. It's a word I associate with comic strips, and she enunciates it just that precisely, so that I can almost see it printed inside a balloon above her head.

There was a time when the thought of remarriage seemed inconceivable to me. I could not wrap my mind around it. When Nandina once or twice referred to it as a possibility for my very distant future, I got a lead weight in my stomach. I felt like someone contemplating food right after a heavy meal. "Oh, that will change, by and by," Nandina said in her all-knowing way. I just glared at her. She had no idea.

The Christmas after she and Gil got engaged, we went to Aunt Selma's for Christmas dinner as usual, except that this year Gil came, too. And as I was driving the three of us over, Nandina just happened to drop the information that Roger and Ann-Marie would be bringing Ann-Marie's girlfriend Louise. I cannot tell you how I dislike the word "girlfriend" when it's used to mean the platonic female friend of a grown woman. Also, I knew perfectly well who this Louise would be. She was the famous Christmas Eve Widow, the one who could presumably have handled her husband's death just fine if he hadn't died just before a holiday. Ah, yes, I could see the machinery spinning here.

"This was supposed to be a *family* occasion," I told Nandina.

"And so it is!" she said blithely.

"I would hardly call the unknown acquaintance of our first cousin's third wife a member of the family."

"Aaron, for mercy's sake! It's Christmas! It's the time for taking in people who have no place else to go."

"What: she's a homeless person?"

"She's, I don't know. Maybe her family lives on the other side of the country. And the season has especially sad connotations for her, if you'll recall."

Notice the careful omission of such telltale phrases as "so much in common" or "getting you two together." But I was no dummy. I knew.

When we arrived at Aunt Selma's, Louise was already in place, installed at one end of the otherwise empty couch. Roger and Ann-Marie sat in armchairs, and Gil and Nandina took the love seat. So, naturally, I was settled next to Louise.

She was what I had expected, more or less: a thin, attractive young woman with a slant of short brown hair that swung artfully to one side when she tipped her head. She tipped her head often during our first few minutes together, fixing me with a bright-eyed gaze as we embarked on the usual small talk. It emerged that she was the type who prefaced even the most unexceptional statement with "Are you sitting down?"—a question I've always compared to laughing at your own jokes. When I asked what she did for a living, for instance: "Are you sitting down?" she said. "I'm an editor! Just like you! Only freelance."

Her thinness was the kind that comes artificially, from dieting. You could tell somehow that she was not the weight that she was meant to be. Her knife blade of a dress had clearly been chosen with an eye to accentuating her prominent collarbones and the two jutting knobs of her hips. I don't know why this annoyed me. I suppose that if we'd liked each other it *wouldn't* have annoyed me, but by now we had both arrived at that despairing stage where you realize that the other person is simply too other to bother with. Louise had stopped prettily tipping her head, and her gaze started veering sideways to conversations elsewhere in the room. I felt a strong urge to excuse myself and go home.

At dinner, she was seated on my right. (We had place cards this year, to ensure there'd be no mistakes.) However, now that she'd given up on me she addressed the bulk of her remarks to Gil, across the table. She announced to him during the soup course that she had a "very unique" relationship with clocks. "Every time I look at one, just about, you know what the time is? Nine-twelve."

Gil said, "Ah . . . ," and wrinkled his forehead.

"And nine-twelve is— Are you sitting down?"

He sent a bewildered glance toward his lap.

"Nine-twelve is the day I was born!"

"Huh?"

"September twelfth! Isn't that just eerie? It happens *way* more often than you can explain scientifically. Why, on my very first trip to London, years and years ago, of course I went to see Big Ben, and can you guess what time it was when I got there?"

Gil looked panicked.

I said, "Twelve-oh-nine?"

"What? No, my birthday is—"

"Because you were in England, after all, where they say 'twelfth September' instead of 'September twelfth.'"

"No . . . actually—"

"Aaron," Nandina broke in, "tell Louise about *Beginner's Jet Lag.*"

"I forget," I said.

"Aaron."

She thought I was being difficult, but I honestly did forget. I couldn't think of anything but the endless number of hours before I could make my escape. Till then, we had so much food to plow through. Not just the soup (cream of flour, as near as I could make out), but baked ham in an overcoat of pineapple rings, olive-drab broccoli, and mashed sweet potatoes cobbled with miniature marshmallows, followed by fruitcake for dessert along with—oh, God—a second dessert, which Louise had brought: a platter of cookies shaped like stars and bells and wreaths. I sent Nandina a "See there?" look, because one thing Nandina hated was unexpected contributions to a dinner party, but she was too mad at me to respond. The cookies were dead-white and paper-thin, dusted on top with red and green sugar. I took one for politeness' sake and bit into it, but it had no taste. Just flat, insipid sweetness. I set it down on my plate and started praying for coffee. Not that I planned to drink any at such an hour, but coffee would signal the end of this interminable meal. It was already late afternoon, and a dull gray twilight furred the corners of the dining room.

In the car as I was driving us home, Nandina gave me a thorough scolding. "Why you can't behave with plain old common garden-variety civility . . ." she told me. She was sitting in the rear, and she leaned so far forward to berate me that her chin was all but resting on the back of my seat. "You were literally looking down your nose at that poor woman!"

"Yes," I said, "and she was looking down *her* nose. Face it, Nandina, we were oil and water. Imagine, a professional editor saying something was 'very unique'!"

"Oh, well, she's only freelance," Nandina said in a milder tone.

Then Gil said, "*Any*how," and asked me if the fog was making driving difficult. He always looked unhappy when Nandina and I quarreled.

I dropped them off at Nandina's with the briefest of goodbyes and drove on. Back home, I changed into comfortable clothes, poured myself a drink, and sat down to read, but I couldn't seem to concentrate. I felt too depressed; I wasn't sure exactly why. Here I'd been longing for home ever since we'd arrived at Aunt Selma's, so shouldn't I feel relieved now?

It occurred to me that secretly, in the murky depths of my subconscious, I had been hoping that Louise and I would like each other.

Between Christmas and New Year's, we closed the office and Nandina went into high gear with the wedding preparations. She accomplished it all in a week: pretty efficient, I *will* say. The ceremony took place on the last day of the year at my parents' old church, which Nandina still attended. I gave her away; her best friend from junior high was matron of honor; Gil's cousin served as best man. The only guests were Aunt Selma and her family, and Gil's three sisters and *their* families, and the Woolcott Publishing staff. Afterward, we held a modest reception at my house, although I didn't have much to do with it. Peggy and the matron of honor saw to the food, and Irene did the decorating, and Roger took charge of the drinks. I was just an innocent bystander.

Then Gil and Nandina went away for a week to the Eastern Shore, which seemed a strange choice in midwinter, but to each his own, I guess. This was traditionally a slow time at the office, so it was no problem doing without Nandina to boss us around. I was editing a new vanity title, *Why I Have Decided to Go On Living*, written by a high-school English teacher. Basically, it was a laundry list of "inspirational" moments, such as *Watching the sky turn orange at night behind the Domino Sugars sign*. I would read choice bits aloud to the others in the outer office. *"Feeling a new baby curl its hand around my index finger,"* I'd call out, and Charles would grunt and Irene would give an absentminded "Sss!" and Peggy would say, "Aww. Well, that *is* a good reason!" They were all so predictable.

Irene flipped through thick magazines that appeared to feature nothing but cosmetics ads. Charles got on the phone and monitored what sounded like very heated quarrels among his daughters, who were still on school holiday while both parents were back at work. Peggy decided to practice touch-typing her numerals and symbols; she said she'd never made it past the standard alphabet keys.

At noon on our last day of freedom, so to speak, we all went out together to the Gobble-Up Café, leaving the office unattended, which theoretically we should not have done, and we ordered wine with lunch, which we almost never did. The Gobble-Up was so unaccustomed to serving alcohol that the wine list read, in its entirety, *Chardonnay $5, Merlot $5, Rosé $4*, and when I asked the waitress, "What is your Merlot?" she said, "It's a red wine?"

I ordered a glass anyway, and the women ordered Chardonnay, and Charles had a beer. Peggy got a bit tipsy on only two sips and told all of us that she thought of us as family. Irene announced that, what the hell, after lunch she was taking off for Nordstrom's winter-coat sale. Charles answered a cell-phone call, contrary to the posted house rules, and waited way too long before he stepped outside, murmuring, "Now, calm down; slow down; you know I can't understand a word when you're crying." And I picked up the whole check, which probably means I was feeling fairly merry myself.

Walking back to the office (bypassing Charles, still on his phone out front), I told Peggy and Irene how unreasonably Nandina had behaved after Christmas dinner. I think that, in my winy flush of good feeling, I imagined that they would express some indignation on my behalf. "She basically ambushes me," I said, "she and Ann-Marie; plunks me next to this woman I have nothing to say to, zero—"

"Oh, now. She was just trying to help," Peggy told me. "She just wants you to find somebody."

There was a time when I would have said, "Find somebody! Who says I *want* somebody?" But on that particular day, still under the influence of my post-Christmas-dinner blues, I didn't bother arguing. All I said was, "Even so. It's not as if losing a spouse were some kind of hobby we could share."

Neither Peggy nor Irene showed the proper empathy, though. Peggy just tsk-tsked, and Irene left us abruptly because by then we'd arrived at our building. "Bye, now," she said, and went off to do her shopping.

"This was a woman so skinny I could have cut a hand on her collarbone," I told Peggy as I opened the door. "She chewed with just her front teeth. She brought cookies made of shirt cardboard."

"You are *mean*," Peggy told me severely. She set her purse on her desk and slipped her coat off.

I hesitated.

"Peggy," I said.

"Hmm?"

"You know your oatmeal-chocolate-chip cookies?"

"Yes."

"Those big, lumpy ones you brought in a while back?"

"What about them?"

"You know how there were bits of things in them? Little crispy bits? Not chocolate chips, not nuts, but something kind of sharp? Like stones?"

"Soy grits," she said. She hung her coat on the coat tree.

"Soy grits," I repeated.

"For the supplemental protein," she said.

Then she said, "Count on you to suspect stones in a gift cookie."

"I didn't say I *suspected* stones. I said they were *like* stones."

"You are so, so wasteful, Aaron," she told me. She settled at her desk.

"I'm what?"

"Anyone else would be *glad* when a person tries to be close. You're too busy checking out her motives."

I said, "Whose motives are you talking about?"

"You can't even see it. You don't even notice. You just let her go to waste."

"Let *who* go to waste?" I asked. "Are you talking about Louise?"

Peggy threw both hands in the air.

"Oh," I said. "Wait."

But she spun toward her computer and started furiously typing. I stood looking at her a moment, and then I walked into my office. I hung my jacket up and settled behind my desk. I didn't return to work, though. I had left my door open and I could still see her—the gilt edging of her ruffled hair beneath the overhead lights, the two waterfalls of white lace flowing from her correctly positioned, dutifully level elbows.

I had known Peggy since we were in first grade; I remembered the extra cubby she'd needed for her stuffed animals. I remembered the pantalettes that had frilled below her skirts in junior high. (Some of our ruder classmates used to call her Bo Peep.) And then of course I knew her from all her talk, talk, talk at the office; bear in mind that she was very fond of talking.

On weekends, she had once told us, she liked to go to Stebbins hardware and ask the gray-haired men who clerked there how to fix a sagging door, or what to do about a curling wallpaper seam. She really did need their advice, she said; but also, she found it a comfort. It took her back to the time when her father was alive.

The present that she gave herself after a trying day was to skip the evening news and watch Fred Astaire movies instead.

And she didn't think her clothes were so odd, she said. (This was in response to a less-than-tactful question from Irene.) They were her way of making an effort—doing something special for the sake of the people around her.

And she took great pleasure in cooking, I knew. She said cooking felt like dancing: it had the same timely moves and the same sense of system and sequence. I could understand that. I pictured her preparing a perfect little meal without a single misstep, humming beneath her breath as she moved around the kitchen. She would arrange a pottery bowl of fresh flowers for the table. She would set out linen napkins that she'd folded into tepees.

I pictured being served such a meal, with the fork at my left and the knife and spoon at my right, instead of all in one hasty clump the way I did it myself. The plate deposited deftly in front of me, positioned exactly so, the fork perhaps moved a bit farther left to make room. The soft warmth of the food rising gently toward my face.

Peggy untying her apron before sitting down across from me.

I got up and went to stand beside her chair. I cleared my throat. I said, "Peggy?"

"What."

"Would you ever be willing to—would you ever like to go out someplace with me?"

Her fingers paused on the keys. She turned and looked up at me.

"Someplace, like, on a date," I said. (In case I hadn't made myself clear.)

She studied me a moment. Then, "Why don't you ask Irene?" she said.

"Irene!"

"I thought Irene was the one you admired so much."

"Oh, well, she was," I said. "She is. But you're the one I'd like to go someplace with."

She went on studying me. I stood a little straighter and tried to look my best. I said, "Couldn't you give me a chance?"

After another long moment, she said, "Well. I could. I would like to give you a chance."

And she did.

. . .

I take Maeve inside for apple juice, and while she's drinking it I settle at the kitchen table with the morning paper. But then Maeve spots my cane leaning beside the back door. She drops her sippy-cup with a clunk and toddles over to grab the cane and bring it to me, like a puppy bringing its leash. "Walk?" she says. "Walk?"

"Finish your apple juice first."

She lets the cane clatter to the floor, abandons it without a glance and picks up her juice and downs it, glug-glug, with her eyes fixed on me the whole time—brown eyes, like mine, but disproportionately large and rayed by sunbeam lashes, like Peggy's. (It always amazes me how two very disparate people's genes can melt together so seamlessly in their offspring.) She slams the cup on the table and claps her hands, all business. "Walk, Daddy," she says.

"Okay, Maevums."

Next door, Mary-Clyde Rust is kneeling in her petunia bed. As we pass she calls, "Morning, Miss Maeve!" and sits back on her heels, clearly prepared for some chitchat, but Maeve waves a hand and keeps going, face set due south, making a beeline for the park. I shrug at Mary-Clyde, and she laughs and returns to her weeding.

The Ushers have a little tin-can trailer in their driveway. Ruth Usher's sister and brother-in-law are visiting from Ohio. Yesterday Maeve was given a tour of the trailer and she was extremely impressed, so I worry she'll insist on stopping today, but she is too intent on getting to the park. The central attraction there is a creek that's good for grubbing around in. I don't think we've ever gone to that park without returning soaked, both of us.

A couple we don't know is approaching—a dark-haired young woman and a young man in a Phillies cap. Maeve is about to zip on by when the man says, "Why, hello there," and she pauses and raises her face to him and flutters her eyelashes, beaming. I've never figured out how she decides which people she'll cotton to. Not two minutes later we meet a jogger who also says hello, and Maeve doesn't give him a glance.

As we're nearing Cold Spring Lane, a car slows instead of passing. I look over to see Nandina's Honda drawing up next to us. "Robbirenna!" Maeve shouts. That's how she refers to the twins when she's excited. (Robby was named for Gil's father; Brenna for our mother.) The two of them survey Maeve stolidly from the backseat, and Nandina leans across to call through the passenger window, "See you at the park?"

"See you," I say.

If it were Gil, he would offer us a ride, but Nandina is a stickler for the child-seat law. She takes off again, and Maeve sits kerplunk on the sidewalk and starts wailing.

"We'll see them in a minute, Maeve."

"See them *now*!"

I reach down for her hand to lift her to her feet. Her hand is a fist, a tight satin knot, and she tries to pull it away, but I keep a firm hold.

Every so often, I reflect on that story Gil told me: how his father came back from the dead to check on Gil's construction work. I know Gil felt it was his father's unfinished business that brought him, but what's occurred to me lately is, couldn't it have been *Gil's* unfinished business? Couldn't Gil have been thinking, *I wish to God I could have settled things with my pop?*

I haven't mentioned this to Gil, though, because I suspect he might be embarrassed he ever told me that story.

Robby and Brenna are older than Maeve by several months, and it shows. They're more reserved, more self-contained, and they have that social presence that day-care centers seem to confer. When we get to the park we find them deeply absorbed in watching a father and son's batting practice—the boy connecting with a solid thwack, his mother and his little sister cheering from the sidelines. "Hi, Robby! Hi, Brenna!" Maeve calls out. They each raise an index finger infinitesimally without taking their eyes from the ballplayers. I feel a tug of pity for Maeve, but she's philosophical about it. She sets off on her own through the weeds along the creek bank. "Butterfly, Daddy!" she calls.

"I see it, honey."

Nandina starts telling me about a dispute she's having with Charles. This has to do with *Why I Have Decided to Go On Living,* which took off a couple of years ago and unexpectedly made its author and us, both, some actual money. In preparation for next Christmas, Charles is proposing a sequel—maybe *Why I Have Decided to Travel More* or *Why I Have Decided to Have Children.* But the author seems to have come down with writer's block, and now Charles is suggesting that we enlist some other author, or even write it in-house. Nandina says, "Am I missing something here? Am I wrong to think that one of those books is enough? Am I hopelessly out of step?"

I say, "No, Nandina, believe me—" and then, "Whoa!" because Maeve has just veered sharply and plunged straight down the bank and into the water. "Get out of there!" I call, and I'm after her in a flash, with Nandina close behind in case I need a hand.

"Turtle, Daddy!" Maeve says. ("Tor-toe," she pronounces it.)

"Get out of there this instant!"

As I'm hauling her up the bank, I see the twins watching us, setting their identical, coin-shaped faces toward us until we're safely on dry land again. Then they turn back to the ballplayers without comment.

Do you imagine it hasn't occurred to me that I might have just made Dorothy's visits up? That they were mere wishful thinking, brought on by the temporary insanity of grief?

But tell me, in that case, how she could have said those things that she knew and I didn't.

That she had refused a better job for my sake.

That she had hidden her feelings for my sake.

In short, that she had loved me.

Did I make *that* up?

On the walk home, Maeve lags and complains. She says her legs are too busy. "You're tired," I interpret for her, but she takes offense at this. "I'm *not* tired!" she says. I get the impression she associates the word "tired" with naps, which she views as torture no matter how much she needs one. I say, "Well, then, maybe you're hungry." This strikes her as more acceptable. It is, in fact, past noon, and I worry that Peggy is waiting lunch for us. But no, as we turn onto our street we catch sight of her up ahead, unloading a final bag of groceries from her trunk. "Mama!" Maeve shouts, and she takes off at a run.

"How was your morning?" Peggy asks her when she's close enough. Maeve just gives her a hug around the knees and races on toward the house. Peggy shuts her trunk lid and waits for me to reach her. "Honestly, Aaron, you're *squelching*!" she says, because my shoes are sopping wet, and so are the cuffs of my trousers. I give her a peck on the cheek and we follow Maeve, who looks as if she's wearing hip boots. Her overalls are dark with creek water from the thighs on down.

My friend Luke told me once that he'd been considering my question about whether the dead ever visit. It was true that I had asked him, back around the time I asked Nate, but this was weeks and weeks later. Apparently he had been deliberating the issue ever since. "I've decided," he said, "that they *don't* visit. But I think if you knew them well enough, if you'd listened to them closely enough while they were still alive, you might be able to imagine what they would tell you even now. So the smart thing to do is, pay attention while they're living. But that's only my opinion."

Well, I have no idea if his opinion was right. But all the same, I'm careful these days to pay attention. I see how Peggy gives a frothy little spin to her skirt as she turns onto our sidewalk, and how Maeve has suddenly, out of nowhere, taught herself to climb steps the grownup way, foot above foot. I make a firm mental note of these things as I follow them into the house.

"What?" Peggy asks in the hall. "What are you smiling at?"

"Nothing."

It would be untruthful to say that I never think of Dorothy anymore. I think of both Dorothys—the one I married and the one who came back to visit. I see the Dorothy I married standing by her office bookcase in her starched white coat, demanding to know what was wrong with my arm, or squinting in a baffled way down the business end of a vacuum-cleaner hose, or fiercely cramming celery into the only Thanksgiving turkey she ever tried to cook. And then I think of how people reacted to the Dorothy who came back—some almost scared and some embarrassed, as if she'd committed a social blunder, and some showing no surprise. But I'm not so sure anymore that those who showed no surprise had forgotten she had died. Maybe they remembered perfectly well. Maybe they were just thinking, *Of course. We go around and around in this world, and here we go again.*

A NOTE ON THE TYPE

This book was set in Adobe Garamond. Designed for the Adobe Corporation by Robert Slimbach, the fonts are based on types first cut by Claude Garamond (c. 1480–1561). Garamond was a pupil of Geoffroy Tory and is believed to have followed the Venetian models, although he introduced a number of important differences, and it is to him that we owe the letter we now know as "old style." He gave to his letters a certain elegance and feeling of movement that won their creator an immediate reputation and the patronage of Francis I of France.